HIGH-RISK
RESCUE

ELIZABETH
GODDARD

LOVE INSPIRED SUSPENSE
INSPIRATIONAL ROMANCE

LOVE INSPIRED® SUSPENSE

INSPIRATIONAL ROMANCE

ISBN-13: 978-1-335-72300-0

High-Risk Rescue

Recycling programs for this product may not exist in your area.

The name of the Lord is a strong tower:
the righteous runneth into it, and is safe.
—*Proverbs* 18:10

To Jesus. Thank you for being my strong tower.

Acknowledgments:

Special thanks to my wonderful editor, Shana Asaro, who believes in my stories and makes them shine brighter. Also, I couldn't do this without the continual encouragement from my writing friends. You know who you are, and you've been there holding me up through the good times and the bad times for going on twenty years! Also, I owe so much to Steve Laube for believing in me early on and pushing me forward. It's hard to believe that you signed me over ten years ago!
The future is bright!

ONE

Hannah Kahn had the strongest sense she was in the wrong place at the wrong time. She wasn't ready to fulfill this role as personal assistant to Alfred Stevens, CEO of Greenco, so soon.

But she'd wanted this, hadn't she? She'd worked hard to land this position and wanted to prove herself. Still, she hadn't counted on Kristen Mayer—the assistant under whom Hannah had been training—to go on maternity leave early when her doctor ordered her to be put on bed rest for the remainder of her pregnancy.

Now Hannah almost felt like she was being set up for failure. Lifting her shoulders, she blew out a breath and banished the ill-timed self-doubts and worries. Forced confidence into her steps and hoped against hope that this newfound conviction would flood the rest of her body. And she needed it to happen *soon*…because as of right now, her clammy palms slicked against the tablet that held her notes and her heart was pounding wildly in her chest as she tried to wrap her mind around the fact that her title had abruptly changed from assistant-in-training to press secretary for this important event.

"A defining day in the life of my company," Mr. Stevens had told her moments before they'd entered the hotel where they would make the announcement.

Yes, she was definitely in the wrong place at the wrong time.

Her heels clicked on the floor as she followed her boss down the hall of the posh convention center slash hotel and through a side door to make his big announcement to the press that Greenco was going public. He'd insisted making a big splash was important to set the stage for the future.

Shadowing them both, the bodyguard hovered near them like a wingman. Mr. Stevens had hired protection and apparently the founder of Honor Protection Specialists himself was providing services.

But of all the people on Planet Earth, why, oh why, did it have to be Ayden Honor? Even her fake confidence had faltered the moment her employer had "introduced" them. Oh, they already knew each other all right. They'd been together and madly in love until she'd broken things off for reasons that she could never tell him.

Ayden's facial expression hadn't changed, but she'd recognized the stunned look in his eyes. The shock and even…anger.

Why did he have to be here today, of *all* days?

He looked better today than when they'd been an item years ago. Maybe a little rougher around the edges—more experience reflected in his deep brown eyes. A tendril of attraction shivered through her. Were his shoulders broader now, or was she seeing things? She sighed inwardly. He still had that strong, stubbled jaw and devastatingly handsome profile, and as her eyes drifted up to take in his thick, dark hair, her heart skipped a beat. She remembered how much she'd loved weaving her fingers through it…

Enough!

Personally knowing the bodyguard didn't do anything to help her feel better about the fact that her boss thought it necessary to hire protection. *Protection*? From what or whom?

The moment she'd been informed that he had employed a bodyguard, her anxiety had ramped up. But Hannah had ample practice in keeping her cool under pressure. Maybe it was like Mr. Stevens had said—one could never be too careful. This was their big day, after all. Hence, he'd recruited Ayden out of an abundance of caution.

Ayden had watched the earlier exchange and Hannah thought she'd read suspicion in his eyes.

He wasn't quite buying into Mr. Stevens's explanation, either. Something about his deep piercing eyes that seemed to see right through her left her unnerved, as if he could tell that she wasn't qualified to be working with this emerging tech company. At least not yet. But worse, her skin crawled with the thought that her ex might be able to see right through her to know what she'd done years ago.

Just breathe… Ayden can't know.

No one knew about what happened except for one other person.

But she shouldn't be wasting precious moments thinking about what she couldn't change. All her focus needed to be on the next few moments of her life that could make or break her future.

She mentally ran through her list of responses to possible questions she could be asked as impromptu press secretary then concentrated on the platform that Mr. Stevens slowly approached. In his midforties, he was a man at the top of his game. Rich and successful. Handsome and happily married. This morning, he cut a striking figure in his black tailored Italian suit and a red power tie. Which seemed fitting for the occasion since he'd made no secret of the fact that he'd been dreaming of and planning for this day for months. Yet while she hadn't known him long, she got the feeling that even Mr. Stevens had a crack in his own confidence. Did the sweat beading at his temples—something she'd never seen on him before—have something to do with the reason he'd hired Ayden? None of that was reassuring.

At the podium, Hannah stood just behind her boss's left shoulder.

Bright lights shined in her eyes, but she resisted the urge to squint and frown, and instead, kept a small curve in her lips. No big smiles just yet. She projected the required confident, quiet professional look and focused on everything the CEO said.

Or tried to…

Her mouth grew dry and her throat tight as nerves fluttered through her once again. She'd wanted an important job… But *behind* the scenes. Not front and center in the midst of the main event.

Alfred Stevens was a charismatic man, and a dynamic speaker. Greenco—a geographic information system software company that would change the future by helping design energy efficient cities, clean water systems and more—was his brainchild that he'd built from the ground up. Now was his day to shine.

That she would be standing next to him seemed surreal. Flicking her eyes to the left, she risked a glimpse at Ayden, who stood in the shadows and out of the limelight, but close enough to act if required. His cool eyes stared at her, measuring her. But she had to be mistaken. Of course he wasn't looking at her specifically. He was looking at everyone. Waiting and watching for possible danger. She obviously happened to glance his way at the same moment he looked at her.

As Mr. Stevens droned on about the path he'd taken to build the company, Hannah directed her attention on the group of invited reporters, as well as the gathered crowd of company employees and public spectators, which appeared larger than she would have expected. But what did she know about press conferences? She was about to get serious on-the-job experience. At least the expressions told her the crowd was congenial rather than antagonistic.

Still… Hannah struggled to shake the sense that she was out of her league.

That voice from the past crept in out of nowhere.

"You're not good enough…"

Why now? God, please help me!

This was her moment to prove herself, and she had to shut down the self-doubt. She had to make her mother proud. After all, she was doing this for Momma as much as herself.

She recalled her mother's words, meant to instill confidence. *You're braver than you believe, stronger than you seem, and smarter than you think...*

Hannah could do this. She was here for a reason. She'd worked hard and she was putting her best professional foot forward.

She should just imagine everyone in the audience wearing clown noses.

Mr. Stevens cleared his throat.

Hannah focused intently on his next words, in which he would announce the company was going public. What came next would be the most challenging part. She would hear question upon question and Mr. Stevens would likely call on her to answer them. She had notes to which she could refer, but she wasn't sure why he'd prepped her for this, since he was here and could respond to those same questions himself. Maybe to generate more buzz and add texture to his news. Or...did he plan to walk out and leave her to deal with the reporters all by herself? At the thought, her heart jumped to her throat.

She was supposed to be an assistant, not a press secretary. But somehow she would make it through this day.

"And now for the reason I gathered you here

this morning. It has been my greatest privilege to build Greenco to what it is today, my greatest honor to work with so many brilliant employees, many of whom I've called friends. But it is with great regret that I…"

Wait. What was he going to say? What could he regret? Uncertainty lodged in her gut, churning up her anxiety.

"I'm…resigning as CEO." His voice croaked out the words as if he hadn't intended them.

The room fell silent.

Cameras flashed, breaking through the bright spotlights shining on Mr. Stevens. Shining on *them both.*

Panic engulfed Hannah. What? He was…resigning? That wasn't what he was supposed to say! She wasn't prepared to answer questions about his resignation.

He turned to look at her, gesturing it was her turn at the podium. His eyes pled with her, and she might have imagined an apology there. Regardless, she remained frozen in place where his words had immobilized her.

She was failing her first test miserably. But it wasn't fair. He hadn't prepared her for this news that clearly stunned everyone.

A shout pulled her out of her dumbfounded state as screams erupted.

"*Bomb!* There's a bomb!"

* * *

Ayden Honor didn't have to think. His experience as a special agent with the US Diplomatic Security Service had primed him to deal with just about anything, but he couldn't deny his shock when someone had shouted that there was a bomb. Or his complete and utter surprise when Hannah Kahn had entered the office and his new client, Alfred Stevens, had introduced his right-hand "man." But Ayden would have to deal with his reaction to seeing Hannah later. *Much later.* All his attention tunneled in around what was happening at this very moment, while his mind scrambled for answers. Had Stevens expected something like a bomb threat to go down? If so, he should have given Ayden a heads-up and been totally honest about the risk factors.

Regardless, his instincts had kicked in even as these unsettling thoughts whirled through his brain.

The crowd of reporters and employees erupted in screams and utter chaos. Gripped with fear and panic, each person was out to save his or her own life and dashed toward one of two exits.

Ayden focused on protecting Mr. Stevens. The man hadn't hired him to specifically protect Hannah, but that came without saying, as far as Ayden was concerned.

Time seemed to slow as he rushed forward

to grab Hannah and Mr. Stevens. Bright green eyes that he'd never forgotten had grown huge and Hannah's mouth hung open. She appeared shell-shocked and just stood there, unmoving, with her long, auburn, perfectly curled hair cascading around her shoulders, as people swelled around her toward the exits at the front and the back of the room. But Stevens had reacted the same—like he was too stunned to move.

The man suddenly snapped out of it and took in the scene as if preparing his escape. Ayden cut across the dais, weaving through those who'd surged toward the exit on this side of the room—the private entrance onto the platform.

He had wanted to stand much closer during the announcement, but the CEO wouldn't have it. The man's decision had now resulted in people swarming around Stevens and Hannah before Ayden could. That would never happen again on his watch. Before Ayden was able to reach them, Stevens turned and grabbed Hannah's hand, showing in that moment that he cared for someone other than himself. But an instant later, Ayden was on them both, seizing their arms and shielding them in a protective stance. He urged them toward the back of the room where, unfortunately, a choke point had formed.

The crowd bottlenecked at the doors, rushing

them, pushing them forward toward the same exit. This was the closest one, and nothing could be gained by trying to go against the grain and head for the other, equally crammed exit across the room.

The bodies crushed around them, even in a crowd of maybe two hundred people or less.

Ayden didn't like being in this position. Not one bit. But he continued to rush Stevens and Hannah forward, while also keeping an eye out for those around him. Someone could have shouted *bomb* to create exactly this kind of scenario and that could put the offender close enough to Stevens to cause bodily harm.

The CEO had to have suspected something like this might transpire.

But Ayden would save his ire for later. Right now, lives were at stake.

The press of bodies was uncomfortable, but worse was not knowing if there was actually a bomb and if there was, when it would go off.

Though he wanted to protect everyone surrounding them, he'd been hired to protect Stevens.

Lord, help me protect others. Guide me!

People pressed in around them, moving toward the door. Hotel alarms blared, ramping up the fear and congestion. Ahead in the hallway, he could see people pouring out of the hotel. Patrons and employees. Some environmental conference was also in play, and those attendees fled as well.

Unfortunately, this was an optimal place to plant a bomb if maximum impact was desired.

A woman fell near the door and cried out for help.

His gut clenched when those behind her didn't stop but instead rushed over her.

"Help her. What's the matter with you?" Ayden barked out to those up ahead.

"We can't stop for her," Stevens said. "I hired you to protect *me*."

"We aren't leaving her." If Ayden stopped to help her, he could risk them all getting hurt, but he couldn't leave her. "We're almost there. I'm going to scoop her up as we go, but we stick together. You hear me?"

Hannah nodded, her terrified eyes focused on the young woman as others continued to disregard her fallen form. Fortunately, she wouldn't have to endure more abuse.

"You're here to shield me, not everyone else!" Stevens growled at Ayden, desperation and fear in his voice.

Ayden gritted his teeth. "Under the circumstances, I will do both."

As the crowd squeezed tighter toward the door, he reached down to lift her up with one arm.

"Can you make it?"

She appeared dazed, battered and bruised, but nodded. "Thank you," she whispered.

They pressed through the exit out into the hallway where more people tried to flee the packed hotel, but it was like rush hour traffic. Slow-going with so many people crammed inside.

Instead of staying with Ayden as instructed, Stevens forced his way through the mob, leaving both Hannah and Ayden behind. She acted as though she wanted to rush forward with her boss then suddenly slinked back and pressed against Ayden. At least she'd stayed with him, but on the other hand, maybe that wasn't by choice. He doubted she had the power to press through the crowd as Stevens had done. He was clearly a man on a mission, determined to save only one life—his own. Stevens had given up on helping Hannah, after all. Still, Ayden was pretty sure everyone here had the same goal.

"Stevens!" Ayden shouted over the crowd, and the blaring alarms, spotting the back of the man's head.

Once through the next door, people spread out and ran toward the two available exits on each end of the long hallway. Ayden had scoped the premises out ahead of time. Through the door across the hall, they would find another exit.

But he'd lost sight of Stevens now. *Great.* The

first client of his new Honor Protection Specialists venture.

"I'm okay. You can let me go," the woman he'd pulled from the floor said, drawing his attention.

"Are you sure?" Hannah touched her arm, impressing him with the fact she was still a kind and caring person in the middle of an everyone-for-themselves atmosphere.

She nodded, glancing between Hannah and Ayden, once he released her to find her own way. Against the wall, she edged her way to freedom.

Panic surged in Hannah's eyes, but to her credit, she remained composed as she looked at him. "Where's Mr. Stevens?"

Ayden gripped her hand and moved through the throng of people rushing from the hotel. "I see him. He's waiting at the back door across the hall."

Odd. But then again, he wouldn't risk leaving the building without his hired bodyguard. And, honestly, Ayden couldn't really be angry at the man for getting himself away safely. He'd made it that far, and no thanks to Ayden.

Still…he didn't want Hannah getting ideas that the danger had passed. They weren't out of the woods yet. "Stick with me." Ayden glanced at her, and she nodded. "As soon as we get out of this hotel, we have to get far away."

"The bomb?"

"Yes." If there was a bomb, it was ticking.

God, please let us get out of here in time. Let these people make it to safety.

At least he served a purpose here today, though a very small one. After this catastrophe, he would be rethinking the kind of clients he took on.

With Hannah in tow, he moved toward the wall then headed away from the main exit and against the tide that fortunately had begun to dissipate as the hotel emptied.

A split second later, gunfire erupted from the front exit. Unleashing panic and pandemonium once again. People who had been fleeing the hotel turned back and ran toward them.

"Hurry!" Ayden rushed Hannah toward the side door in the hallway that would lead to another exit.

Stevens waited for them at the door—Ayden had gone over the exits with him should they need one—and the CEO stared at Ayden now, willing him forward as if his life depended on it.

He suddenly slid down, leaving a streak of blood on the wall.

"Stevens!" The sight gutted Ayden and when he reached him, he crouched next to the dying man.

Hannah screamed and dropped to her knees

next to her boss. "Mr. Stevens! No, no, no, Alfred."

Ayden took in the scene before him. Found the man's midsection already drenched in blood. He assessed Stevens's injuries, but in his peripheral vision he caught Hannah's tear-filled eyes, along with the accusing look she gave Ayden. Her grief shifted to anger.

The injured man's pulse was weak and erratic and then…gone. He'd lost too much blood already and there was nothing Ayden could do to help him now.

But he could help get Hannah to safety.

Another round of gunfire suddenly erupted then the wall near her head took a bullet.

Hannah pressed her hands over her ears and squeezed her eyes shut. She curled into a ball against the wall and prayed this nightmare would go away. More gunfire ensued, close enough she felt it to her bones. She couldn't breathe.

I'm going to die!

Ayden crouched next to her, covering her, *protecting* her. If only Mr. Stevens had stayed with him, he might be alive. When Hannah opened her eyes, Ayden aimed his gun and then fired at their shooter as people continued frantically clearing the hallway. Keeping his gun ready to shoot, he gripped her arm. His handsome face suddenly filled her vision, his eyes penetrating. Ayden's mouth moved, but she couldn't comprehend the words. Then his deep frown, the fierce determination in his gaze, broke through her paralyzed mind as she took in what he said and what he meant.

"We. Have. To. Run!"

He tugged on her arm, forcing her up from the floor, then pulled her away from Mr. Stevens. She took in his motionless body and wished she hadn't. She would never be able to erase that image from her mind.

Alfred.

He was gone now.

Gone!

She stared at his lifeless eyes again as if that would help her to grasp this new reality, but her mind couldn't gain traction and she remained dumbfounded. Ayden's shouts carried through a wave of screams as hotel security guards rushed in to protect people against the shooters.

Ayden lifted her off her feet with one arm and carried her. "Someone shot at you! We need to go if you don't want to end up dead like your boss."

"But Mr. Stevens! We can't just leave him."

She twisted around to look at Alfred's body one last time. *God...* But there was nothing she could pray, nothing she could do for him now.

"He's gone." Ayden dropped her down to her own feet, releasing her to run with him, which she did. "We're going through the door. Stevens was waiting for us to get through to the exit here."

"And he got shot while waiting for us."

Ayden's grip tightened. "I'll protect you."

"You weren't hired to protect me. You were hired to protect…" What was she saying? That she didn't want his help? Ayden hadn't succeeded in safeguarding Mr. Stevens, but she wouldn't bring that up now. He already knew. "Okay. Let's go."

Using his body as a shield, he ushered her to the door. His back to her, he held his weapon ready to lay down cover if necessary. "Open it."

She grabbed the handle and twisted. Nothing. She pulled but it didn't budge. "It's locked!"

"Stand back."

She moved out of the way but kept to the shadows of the small alcove. Ayden somehow managed to keep her covered, as he kicked the door repeatedly. It finally gave way with a reverberating thud.

A bullet whizzed by her head, plunking in the Sheetrock.

Screaming, she ducked.

"Keep going down the hallway."

He didn't need to tell her twice. This time,

anyway. She finally pushed back the paralyzing fear and vowed to keep moving. She ran through the doorway and continued down a long hallway, Ayden behind her. "Where are we going?"

"Hang a right. There should be an exit."

Gasping for breath, fueled by fear, she ran down the long corridor, feeling like it just kept getting longer. Finally, she made it around the corner and took a right as he instructed. A brightly lit exit showed the way.

Hannah hesitated before going through. "But… What if they're waiting on us?"

"I'm going first to clear the garage."

"This leads to the parking garage?" She imagined Mr. Stevens had arranged to have a car waiting. But that wasn't going to help them now. His driver had dropped them all off, and she had no clue where he was now.

She studied Ayden while also listening for the sound of pounding feet in the hallway, the only warning they would likely get if they had been followed.

Sweat beading on his brow, Ayden nodded and brandished his gun. "Wait for my signal." He left her standing there alone when he exited.

She hadn't realized how much his mere presence projected protection. And maybe that's why Mr. Stevens had died—he'd ran ahead and left Ayden's side. Maybe the bodyguard's presence alone warded off evil. And with that thought she realized she'd rather be next to Ayden—despite the awkwardness of their past—than hiding in a lonely hallway during a bomb threat and shootout. Heart pounding, she feared those who had started the deadly rampage would come running after her. They had to have seen her and Ayden exit this way, of course, because they'd landed a few near misses at her head.

She started inching toward the exit despite his warning to wait. A breath away from her rushing through that door to join him in the parking garage, Ayden returned. And like she'd hoped, his appearance calmed her—if only a little.

Though she never wanted to see him again after their relationship ended, he was the security guy in this awful scenario, and she was grateful for his skills and protection.

"The garage is clear for the moment," he said. "Let's go. Stay behind me. *Close* behind me. Understood?"

"Yes."

Together they hurried through the door, stuck to the walls and then he led her around the corner. Tires squealed.

Her heart rate skyrocketed at the threatening sounds—a vehicle steered by bad guys bent on getting to her rather than exiting with the threat of a bomb?

Oh, Lord...

Running through the hotel, herded by shooters down hallways and into the garage, she'd forgotten about the bomb. It was too much to keep up with.

"Change of plans." The coarse timbre of Ayden's voice rumbled through her, setting her teeth on edge.

"What?" She moved behind a support beam for cover.

"We're not going through the garage," he said. "We have to backtrack. Head for the stairwell."

She inwardly groaned. "But that will take us back into the building."

"And away from the attackers. Your pursuers."

Your pursuers. "Why would anyone pursue me? I'm a nobody!"

She hadn't expected a reply and all she got was his well-calibrated machine of a body rushing her through another door, while shielding her. Would he really take a bullet for her? She couldn't fathom anyone would lay down their life for someone else.

Though, she knew One who'd paid the highest price for them all.

Ayden led her downstairs, moving slower than he normally would have, she suspected, so that she could keep up.

Even so, she gasped for breath—the heightened activity along with fear squeezing her heart and lungs. "Where are we going now?" She asked the question on a gasp.

"Out another exit."

"You know about this how?" she asked.

"My job to scope out the place."

Had it also been his job to look for potential bomb hazards? She bit back the question.

Both of them were breathing hard by the time they made it down to another floor that exited out into a loading dock area.

He edged toward the exit where an idling truck waited. Forgotten as someone fled the area?

"We have to hurry before someone attempts to stop us here." Ayden rushed past the truck and into the alley.

"Wait! What are you doing? We could just climb into this truck and escape that way."

"And draw too much attention. No, let's stick with my plan." He checked the alley, looking both ways, then gestured across the way. "We're going to head into that building across the street."

She wouldn't argue with a protection expert who held her life in his hands, but if it had been left up to her, she would have driven the truck out of here. Then of course they might have been pursued by her "pursuers," whoever they were. Okay. So he knew what he was doing.

Sirens rang out, bouncing off the walls between the buildings, reminding her that everyone was in danger, not just her.

God, please let everyone make it out of the hotel!

Images of Mr. Stevens accosted her, but she had to survive to tell her story. To tell *his* story.

A protective arm at her waist, gun at the ready, Ayden ushered her across the alley and through a door that easily pushed open. A side door like this she fully expected to be locked.

The loud honk and rumble of an engine echoed against the brick walls, and she saw a flash of red before the door closed.

A fire truck. Probably more than one.

Inside the building, Ayden broke through yet another door and entered another stairwell. At a landing between floors, he stopped to wipe his brow, then turned his dark eyes on her.

She remembered those eyes so well, and the look he'd given her when she last saw him— one of the most painful, heartbreaking days of her life.

"We'll wait here until help arrives." His voice was gruff as he scraped his free hand down his face.

She never would have dreamed she would be stuck in a small space with Ayden Honor again. Memories rushed at her from the past and entangled with their present predicament. Dizziness swept over her.

"Are you okay?" He reached forward as if to steady her.

She took a step back, and instantly regretted it when she saw the anger and hurt flash in his eyes. He wasn't the enemy now. He wasn't the enemy back then, either. "I—I'm fine, thanks. I heard sirens. Sounds like help is here."

"They're here to address the bomb threat first, and gunfire if it continues. I suspect since the target has been removed, the shooting has ceased."

Target. He meant her. How could it be her?

When she didn't say anything, he continued, "Don't worry. You're safe at the moment."

Huffing out a breath, Ayden paced the small landing, and Hannah backed up against the wall. She didn't mind the support, and the small space it gave her from Ayden.

"We'll talk to the police at some point. But right now, I need to keep you safe." He said the words as if reassuring himself.

"Mr. Stevens didn't hire you to keep me safe. To me that means I shouldn't be a target or else he would have hired you to keep me safe, too."

"Right now, you're an extension of Stevens. It's obvious you were targeted, too. I'm going to need your phone."

"My phone?"

"Need to make sure it isn't being tracked."

Hannah fished it out of her pocket and handed it over. She was actually surprised she still had it because she'd lost her iPad in the chaos. Maybe she'd placed it on the podium, but she couldn't remember what happened.

Ayden examined her phone and then all he did was turn it off. He stuffed it in his pocket. "As far as who he hired me to protect—do you really think I would leave you unprotected, regardless?"

In his eyes, she saw a thousand emotions swell, and she wasn't sure she wanted to answer that question. Was he protecting her because of their past history? Or because he was just a good guy? A hero. She'd bet the latter.

Broad shoulders lifted, his feet spread in a wide stance, he held his gun at his side. She had no doubt that he was a skilled marksman. Feeling his penetrating gaze, she slowly lifted her eyes to meet his. The way he looked at her now, she had the distinct sensation he was peering right into her soul.

And she knew Ayden wouldn't leave her unprotected, under *any* circumstance.

"No. I don't."

Her emerald green eyes sparked with trust, which honestly surprised him. But it also reassured him. Especially since her boss had hired Ayden and he'd failed to protect the man. Given what happened between Hannah and Ayden nine years ago, he wasn't sure what to expect from her. This was uncharted territory for them both.

When she'd broken things off with him—on the day he had meant to propose—he'd seen fear and mistrust in her tear-filled eyes. That look had startled him, cut him to the quick. Where had it come from? What had happened? He must have done something to cause her pain, but he had no idea what it could have been. And protecting her now, this woman he'd once loved, was also a huge distraction for him.

He didn't think Hannah's presence, the effect she had on him, had anything to do with Stevens's death, though. At least he hoped not, and he pushed the doubt aside. He couldn't afford it right now.

Ayden fisted his free hand and wanted to pound it into the wall.

Stevens, why didn't you listen? Why didn't you stick close?

What was worse—he wasn't sure that even if Stevens had been right by his side, that he would still be alive. Ayden prided himself on his years of experience keeping high-risk assets safe in the US Diplomatic Security Service. But he'd left that all behind and preferred keeping things low-key in his new endeavor—Honor Protection Specialists.

Right.

Today had been anything but low-key.

Anguish and rage twisted inside of him. Still, he maintained his composure in front of Hannah.

Leaning against the wall, she stared at the floor—to avoid looking at him, he was sure—and hugged herself. What was she thinking? That hiring him hadn't done her boss any good? She'd be well within her rights to have those thoughts.

Ayden ground his teeth together. He still wanted to slam his fist into the wall, but right now he had to exhibit control over his emotions. This dangerous situation wasn't over yet.

He could berate himself when the dust settled, but right now—with a dead client—he wasn't exactly sure when that would be.

Earlier, while he'd been clearing the garage and Hannah had waited for him in the hall, he'd contacted his sister, Everly, who worked with him at HPS. She was heading this way. Together, they would do everything in their power to make sure Hannah was safe.

"What can you tell me about what happened today?"

Her mouth dropped open. "Me? I know less than you do."

"You worked as his assistant. He introduced you as his right-hand 'man.' Why did he hire me?"

Though he'd kept his tone even and his voice gentle, she took a step back, as if his questions were an affront, but he needed the truth.

"I told you I don't know anything. I was surprised to see you in his office today. And not because it was you. Though that surprised me, too. I was surprised because this was the first I knew he'd hired protection. Honestly, it made me nervous. Again, not because it was *you*, Ayden, but because...why would he need protection?"

"Why would Stevens enlisting my services make you nervous?" Did she have something to hide? He wasn't being fair. A bodyguard's job was to make people uncomfortable.

"Not you personally. I just wasn't ready to step into the full responsibility as his assistant. And I especially didn't realize the job would come with danger."

"Do you have any ideas about from where that danger might have come?"

She lifted her chin. "I told you I know nothing. I only meant the fact he had hired you meant he thought there could be danger. Although he reassured us both he was just being cautious."

Just being cautious... Why?

Maybe Hannah knew something she wasn't

sharing, maybe she didn't. But in any event, he wouldn't press her more just yet.

Sighing, he crossed his arms and glanced at his watch. Everly would be pulling up soon so they could jump into the vehicle and get out of here.

One thing he knew, Alfred Stevens had hired him without being transparent about what he truly feared. He made it out to sound like he felt he needed protection from possibly being overwhelmed by reporters over his big announcement. At first, Ayden considered not taking Stevens on since his situation hadn't appeared to involve any real sense of danger or threat.

But he had made his first mistake. He'd been overeager for that first client.

Regardless, Ayden had never let his guard down for a moment. Still, either this was a strange random coincidence or Stevens had left him in the dark about what or whom he was up against, and Stevens had been targeted.

A bomb threat.

Armed gunmen.

Chaos, and now his client lying dead in a pool of blood.

Sniffles drew his gaze back to Hannah, who'd taken a seat on the steps.

Had the additional gunshots truly been meant for her? Had she been specifically targeted?

Since a bullet had come close to claiming her more than once, she was in jeopardy too and all this obviously came as a shock to her. Seeing her boss murdered was a rough experience.

But it came as a shock to him, too. Seeing Hannah today for the first time in nine years, his heart had thumped against his ribcage, and it took all his energy to remain composed. Aloof. Professional. This woman had been the catalyst to send him across the country to DC where he ended up working for the DSS.

Did she know how much power she once held over him?

A muscle ticked in his jaw. The past was the past, and he couldn't let it get in the way of the job he had to do right now.

He stepped closer then crouched in front of her and drew her chin up. He steeled himself against the effect her luminous eyes had always had on him, and even now mesmerized him despite his effort to resist. When he saw her again today, he hadn't been able to keep his gaze off her, which wasn't good in his line of business. He needed to remain professionally detached per his training.

But that training hadn't included facing the person who had shattered his heart.

Her appearance today had surprised him and thrown him off his game. But that wasn't on her, and he would finish this. Though Hannah was strong and capable, that didn't diminish the frightened look in her eyes.

And his protective instincts ramped up.

"This is going to sound strange, under the circumstances, but…how are you doing?"

Her face scrunched in surprise.

"Please, I need to know—are you hurt?"

She shook her head, but he knew it wasn't true. He could tell she was hurting on the inside—psychologically—if not physically.

All he could think to say was, "This will be over soon."

And that sounded even stranger than what he'd said before.

"No. I don't think it will."

TWO

Oh, why had she blurted that out?

Suspicion grew in his eyes, and he stood, then took two steps back on the landing. "Why do you say that?"

Exactly.

His startled reaction now reminded her of that moment she'd broken up with him. Pushing those memories aside, she squeezed her eyes shut and drew in a calming breath. Their shared past had no business dropping in here and now. She could keep reminding herself that. But focusing on this life-and-death situation helped. She, too, wanted to know the answer to why she'd said those words.

She rose from the steps and thrust her fingers through her tangled hair. She must look a mess—but what did she care?

"I don't know, okay?" She just wanted to get out of this stairwell. "What's happening out there? Can we go now?"

She hoped she'd managed to redirect his thoughts.

"I'll answer that, when you tell me why you said you don't think it's over."

Hannah thrust her hands up in the air. "Come on! We both know you said the words you said to comfort me. Nothing more. It's not going to be over soon, and we both know it."

He nodded, seemingly satisfied with her answer.

"We're safe here. Just a few more minutes and we're getting out of here. But I still want to know why you don't think it'll be over soon."

She blew out a frustrated breath. He wasn't going to let it drop, and he hadn't bought her answer like she'd thought. Now wasn't the time to shrink under pressure. "All right. I can't know for sure, but it's just a gut feeling."

He fisted his hands on his hips. His broad shoulders, strong biceps, capable hands and those piercing dark eyes should intimidate her, but they didn't.

"Honestly," he said, "when I said this would be over soon, I meant our current predicament in the stairwell. But your response… You were referring to something more."

"Yes, I was. But let's not beat a dead horse." Okay, now she was just putting her foot in her mouth. But what happened today was…incomprehensible.

He scratched his scruffy jaw. "Fine, but Hannah, you must know something. After all, you said you were being trained to be his clone. Even what seems like nothing could be something. And if you don't want to tell me, then tell the police."

An uncontrollable shudder ran through her, and she turned her back on the man who still managed to rattle her.

Then something hit her. She turned to face him again.

"Wait. There *is* something. Mr. Stevens had planned to announce the company was going public."

His features darkened. "I'm glad you brought that up. I was surprised to hear he would call a press conference to announce he was resigning, but to each his own. Did you know he planned to resign?"

She shook her head vehemently. "No. Not at all. I'm surprised by everything that happened today."

His hands suddenly pressed gently against her upper arms, and he leaned in close. "I'm sorry. I didn't mean to upset you. I know this has been a rough day. I won't press you on it anymore. Thanks for sharing at least that much with me.

We'll figure it out. But right now, time to get out of here."

We'll figure it out? "Where exactly are you taking me?"

"Away from here. I won't know more about your safety until I know more about the threat."

His gun out, he tugged her behind him and opened the door. He peeked out first, looking in all directions. A sporty silver SUV sped through the alley and stopped at the door he held open. He ushered Hannah through the door, quickly opened the door to the vehicle's back seat, and she scrambled inside, glad to be getting out of the stairwell. Though apprehension squeezed her chest.

He climbed into the front passenger seat next to the woman driving. "Go."

The SUV crawled through the alley and turned left at the corner, away from the barricades. "Hannah Kahn, meet Everly Honor."

"Honor? She's your—"

"Sister. That's right. She works with me at HPS."

Hannah hadn't met Ayden's siblings before. She'd only interacted with his parents. Did Everly hold animosity toward her because of what happened? If she did, it didn't show as she smiled at Hannah in the rearview mirror. Everly's eyes were more hazel, whereas Ayden's were dark brown, and her shoulder-length brown hair was pulled into a ponytail. Though Ayden hadn't told her much about his siblings, she knew that he was the oldest at thirty-two.

Relaxing a bit, she let her head rest against the seat back as they headed away from the hotel in West Ridge, a city a few miles southeast of Tacoma but west of Mt. Rainier. Down one street she caught a glimpse of barricades and emergency vehicles. "The building is still there. I'm guessing there was no bomb."

"The bomb threat is still a danger until they've searched the entire building," Everly said.

Hannah watched the scenery pass them by. She wanted to ask where they were going, but she didn't have the energy. Mr. Stevens was gone. Her new boss had been *killed*. She had to hold it together and not lose it in front of Ayden and his sister. He was practically a stranger now. And a bodyguard? Protection services? When had that happened? When she'd known him before, he was a senior at the University of Washington—and she was a freshman. A lot could happen in nine years, and they were both different people now. So yeah, he was a stranger.

"My brothers, Brett and Caine, are part of HPS too."

Why tell her? Hannah figured he was simply trying to get her mind off what had happened.

Okay. She could play along. Maybe that would help. "What do you do, Everly?" Hannah asked.

The woman flicked her gaze to Ayden as if asking his permission, but he didn't respond.

"Anything Ayden needs me to do."

Okay, well that told her a lot.

"And your brothers?"

"Same," Ayden said. "Maybe you'll get to meet them."

Uncomfortable, Hannah shifted in the seat. "And why would I meet them?" It wasn't like he was taking her home to meet the family, and yet, this felt oddly familiar. He'd taken her to meet his parents and that had been a bad idea.

"Because we're going to the HPS offices," Everly said. "Brett and Caine are both there."

Hannah sat up and Ayden peered over his shoulder as if in answer to her silent question. His gaze softened, reassurance surging in his eyes. "Until we learn more, it's the best place."

"What about going to the police?"

Everly glanced at Hannah in the rearview mirror. "They'll come to us."

Wow. Okay. Hannah pushed away the mental fog—what did she really know about Ayden Honor's life now? Or for that matter, his sister? She clenched the hand rest. How much could she trust them, if at all?

Everly steered the SUV around what looked

like an old warehouse. In the back, a wide door automatically opened, and the vehicle headed into a dimly lit parking garage.

Wariness crawled through her for not the first time today. "Where are we?"

"Don't worry, Hannah. It's the safest place for you right now until we get a few things sorted out." Ayden spoke so gently she almost didn't recognize his voice.

Then again, she *did* recognize it—he'd spoken softly to her *before*, whispering his love to her. His softness now seemed out of place, considering the professional and tough bodyguard demeanor that he'd projected since she'd first seen him in Mr. Stevens's office.

Hannah unbuckled, but Ayden was already hurrying around to open the door for her. She stepped out and looked around the space—a typical parking garage, except it was mostly empty, but for three vehicles including the one Everly had driven. Ayden's sister gave her a warm smile. The woman was smallish but with a tough and capable bearing, not unlike Ayden. Still her hazel eyes were kind and caring.

Who are you people? She knew something of Ayden and his family, and more than she wanted to know of his father, Judge Pierson Honor. Looked like she was about to find out much more.

"Come on. Let's get you inside, safe and sound." Everly gestured for Hannah to follow Ayden to a door that required his handprint before it would open.

She stiffened and slowed to a stop.

"What's the matter?" the other woman asked.

"I… I don't know…"

Everly took both her hands in her own and stared at her. "Look, I understand. You've had a big shock today and probably aren't sure who you can trust. But…you already know Ayden, Hannah. And you trusted him. Whatever happened between you two before isn't at play here today. We're just trying to protect you. Will you allow us to do that?"

"I… I want to." She straightened her shoulders and prepared to hold her ground. She had been assistant to Alfred Stevens, after all.

Her mother's words came back to her. *You're braver than you believe, stronger than you seem and smarter than you think…*

"I'll give you a reason to trust us." A hint of impatience edged Everly's voice. "Ayden just saved your life, and he isn't done yet. The police are on their way here. A detective is going to take your statement. Look, all we want to do is protect you. You're free to walk away."

"Just like that." Hannah held Everly's gaze.

Ayden's sister released Hannah's hands to cross her arms. "Yes. Just like that."

Hannah could think of no good reason not to trust them. Well, then again, she could think of one—Judge Honor—but maybe she was being too harsh to think Ayden and his sister were anything like their father. Besides, the man was dead. If she walked away, she would go home but she needed to understand where the danger was coming from, and that was all Ayden and his sister were trying to do.

Protect her. Like she was trying to protect—

Mom... Oh, Mom! "I need to call my mother. She's probably freaking out about what happened!" She stepped away from Everly. She was free to walk away, wasn't she? Oh, that's right. Ayden had taken her cell from her.

She was trapped, after all.

Ayden held the door open for Hannah, waiting for her to walk through, but she remained wary. He didn't like being part of the reason she was upset or distrusting. His goal and mantra for his business was to serve and protect.

Hannah fisted her hands. "I need to talk to my mother. She's probably worried. Please, give me my phone back."

He fished it out of his pocket, turned it on and handed it over. Ayden had never met Hannah's mother when they were dating. He got the feeling Hannah hadn't wanted him to meet her, and yet he knew she loved the woman. She spoke of her often. She never talked of her father though, so he suspected something had happened there. Then one day after she'd ended their relationship, he'd followed her home. Like a stalker, he'd wanted to know if she'd been seeing someone else, and if that had been the reason why she'd broken things off. Because her breakup had made zero sense.

She'd loved him. He'd *known* she'd loved him.

He'd been completely blindsided. So he'd followed her to a small home in one of the poorer neighborhoods. The house had been in desperate need of a coat of paint and, he could easily see by the way the porch leaned, some major structural work. If he had known, if she had invited him into that part of her life, he would have been there in a moment. Painting and doing the needed work. He'd loved her. He would have loved her mother. He would have done anything for her.

"What are you doing? That could—" His sister's harsh words brought his mind back to the moment.

"I need her to trust us."

Everly's eyes narrowed, but Hannah blinked

up at him, then she took the phone and stared at the screen. "I don't have a signal."

He'd known, of course, when he turned it on that she would get no signal, and that she would be in no immediate danger of being tracked.

"Not down here, no," he said. "If someone is tracking you that cell could give your location away."

"Then let me use *your* cell phone or some other way to contact her. You don't understand. She's…sick."

The pain in her voice squeezed his chest.

"Fine," Everly said. "Just please turn your cell off for now, okay?"

Hannah nodded, powered it down and stuck it in her pocket. Ayden hoped he could trust her to keep it turned off. He had already experienced one debacle today that had ended in his client's death. His gut still churned with the images and the failure.

"You can make the call from a secure cell," he said. "You'll probably have your life back soon and be able to turn your cell on without fear of being tracked. The sooner we get inside and debrief, the sooner this will be over."

Right. Over. This was a long way from over except regarding his protection services business—HPS could already be dead before it even had a real chance.

He gestured for her to walk through the door. Hannah sighed and her shoulders dropped as if she hadn't been happy about accepting his terms, but she went inside ahead of him all the same. Her green eyes flicked to him briefly as she passed. He caught a whiff of coconut shampoo that he'd somehow missed in all the chaos. Not that he needed to be thinking about the scent of her shampoo.

Everly passed by and gave him a look that held a thousand warnings. Behind the two women, he scraped a hand down his face as he closed and secured the door.

His sister led Hannah up another stairwell onto the main floor that housed their offices. Maybe once Hannah learned to trust them, and Ayden trusted her, as well, he would give her a tour of the facilities, which included the latest surveillance and counterintelligence technology, a full gym, living area and kitchen, as well as sleeping quarters for each of them. Additional space had been secured for guests as a temporary safe house as needed. He'd tried to prepare for every eventuality, because once he got this up and running, he didn't want to pause operations in order to build or add on, though that, too, was inevitable.

Ayden had put all his savings into this business start-up, running with the assumption that

Honor Protection Specialists would grow and thrive. Or rather, he'd had faith it would grow. And why shouldn't it grow?

He hadn't anticipated what could go painfully wrong, and today's turn of events had flipped all his dreams and his future on their head. But a man was dead, and he wouldn't let thoughts of his business aspirations, or even his past romantic failure, take priority in his thoughts.

Everly eyed him then pressed a hand on Hannah's arm. "I got this. We're going to freshen up. Detective Mann should be here any minute."

Ayden nodded, giving his approval for the much-needed break. He headed to his office and dropped into his ergonomic chair behind a functional executive desk. Monitors on the wall showed the events as they unfolded in the news. Elbows on his desk, he pressed his head in his hands.

Why, God?

He couldn't take his mind off the image of Alfred Stevens's body. His blood-soaked shirt.

A light knock came at the door. He wasn't ready to face anyone, but it was probably his sister letting him know the investigator was here. In his business, he already had relationships with the local law enforcement agencies. Mom and Dad had both been about justice—his father a judge, and his mother a special agent.

Both had been killed on the job while Ayden had been far from here, working in the DSS on the other side of the world. But now he was back, and all he wanted was to live up to their reputations. Their legacies of justice. But in his *own* way.

After the knock came again, Ayden finally said, "Come in."

The door opened wide and both his brothers, Brett and Caine, entered, each looking as haggard as Ayden felt. While both Ayden and Everly had taken after Mom, who had dark hair and more of an olive complexion, Brett and Caine had lighter complexions and hair. Younger than Ayden, they'd both had stints in the military, and he was glad they were both home safe and sound, and willing to work with him in this new endeavor.

"It was a bogus bomb threat," Brett said, clasping his hand on his head.

"Someone wanted to create chaos," Caine muttered. "Why?"

Ayden stared at a painting of David and Goliath on the wall. "So Alfred Stevens could be taken out."

"There were easier ways to do it." Brett crossed his arms and plopped on the sofa against the wall under the painting.

"I took one of the shooters out. But was anyone else shot?" Ayden asked. "I heard gunfire but didn't see."

"Two others. They're being treated at the hospital."

"Find out more about the victims," Ayden told his brothers.

"You're thinking this could be about someone other than Alfred Stevens?" Brett murmured.

"Maybe. Not sure. Stevens brought me in yesterday. I know I should have turned it down. But it was supposed to be simple press conference with nothing going on in the background. Obviously, he wasn't up front with me about his concerns, and today's pandemonium confirmed that. But you're right, maybe this wasn't about him. There was an environmental conference going on at the same time as his scheduled press conference."

"And Hannah Kahn?" Brett asked.

"She could simply have been collateral damage, if she'd been taken out, too," Caine said.

"Or she could be a target." Ayden rose and paced the space behind his desk.

Brett gave an incredulous laugh. "I mean, why is your ex in the middle of this?"

"How should I know?" Ayden bit out.

"Look. Never mind that. What's our policy going to be, man?" Brett asked. "Every time a protection job goes south, do we spend resources investigating?"

"You're suggesting we let it go?" Ayden stopped pacing to stare his brothers down.

"Not at all. But…" Caine shared a look with Brett.

Great, they were teaming up against him.

"This wasn't supposed to happen. I never expected this to *go south*, as you put it." Way to keep stating the obvious. He had a feeling that Hannah, who he hadn't been specifically hired to protect, was going to complicate matters. He'd made a career in criminal investigations, counterintelligence, cybersecurity and threat analysis. Protection meant a lot more than simply showing up as muscle.

Whatever keeping Hannah safe entailed, Ayden vowed to do. And he would find the truth about what had happened.

THREE

In the restroom off the small conference room where Everly had taken her, Hannah stared at herself in the mirror. Her hair had been perfect and her makeup just right, with expectations she would share some of the limelight with her boss. At least the day had started out that way. Now... Her auburn locks were a tousled mop. Her waterproof mascara had somehow smudged, and what happened to her blush and lipstick? They were all gone, and a pale, plain woman stared back at her in the mirror.

Oh, no...was that a smudge of *blood* at her temple? She turned the faucet on, intending to scrub it off. It had to be Mr. Stevens's blood. Why hadn't Ayden told her she had it on her face? A jumble of emotions rushed through her in waves. She'd give anything to take a long, hot shower right now and scrub away the blood, the dirt and grime, and...the pain.

If only it were that easy. And she couldn't take

a shower because she needed to answer questions, and she'd better mentally prepare for that. Emotionally, too. She was an absolute wreck both inside and out.

She took a few calming breaths. Scrubbed at her temple with a damp cloth, then washed the blood from her hands.

Mr. Stevens's blood.

Everly had given her a shirt to change into and had stashed her bloodstained blouse in an evidence bag. The HPS-emblemed golf shirt donned, she splashed water on her face and finger-combed her hair before she noticed a small plastic toilet bag on the counter. Wow, her thoughts were seriously distracted if she hadn't seen it earlier. She unzipped it and found a disposable toothbrush and toothpaste, a hairbrush, lip balm, soap and more. She released a long exhale and felt the fight go out of her.

As if the adrenaline was bleeding out of her.

Just how often did they expect to have guests in Hannah's situation? Then again, Everly had thought things through, and was obviously being considerate.

She'd give Ayden's sister that.

After brushing her teeth and combing her hair, she felt presentable. Though now that she thought about it, the detective seeing her in her former distraught state might come across more convincing, in case he doubted her.

Then it hit her. Everly looked like she'd been on her cell phone, but really, she'd been taking photographs of Hannah covered in blood.

Exiting the restroom, she closed the room behind her and found a soda and small bag of crackers on the coffee table. Everly had left her alone to relax in a small quiet room with a comfy sofa and chair. An *interrogation* room, HPS style? Hannah couldn't complain. And if she and Everly had met another time and place, maybe they could have been friends. Regardless, Ayden's sister had meant to give Hannah a chance to calm down before the investigators got there to ask questions. She had assumed their preferred methods meant interviewing witnesses and victims while they remained at the scene. But that simply wasn't possible today.

At least Everly had given her an untraceable cell so that Hannah could call her mother.

To that end, she closed her eyes and drew in a few breaths.

Just. Calm. Down.

Her efforts didn't work since her hands trembled. Still, she would try to steady her nerves. Momma would worry because she would easily be able to pick up on the fear and the stress in Hannah's voice.

Then again, if Momma watched the news, she would be terrified regardless of what Hannah said or how she said it. And she couldn't leave her mother wondering what had happened to her, no matter if her voice sounded shaky or not.

She dialed Momma's cell and it went to voice mail.

Come on, Momma. Answer, please.

Hanging her head, Hannah tried to steady her breath as she tried again. She struggled to push the images out of her head. But she would need those images, those memories to answer the detective's questions.

"Hello? Who is this?"

Ah. That made sense. Momma hadn't recognized the number.

"Momma, it's me. I'm okay." She let the words rush out before her mother could worry one more second. Tears choked out the rest of what she might have said.

"Oh, Hannah." Momma's words came out breathless. "I was so worried. Where are you? What happened? You were supposed to have your big day and then I saw on the news…"

"Momma, please calm down. I needed to call you to tell you that I was okay. I don't know anything, and right now I'm waiting to give the police my statement about what happened."

"Are you safe?" Her mother's voice croaked with tears now. "People were shot."

The bloody images accosted her again. "Yes, Momma."

God, please let me be safe. But she wouldn't give her mother another reason to fret.

"I'll come down to the police station to get you."

"No," she said a little too loudly. "No, Momma. Please, I don't want to worry about you. Just stay home. I'll come to you as soon as I can. But there are a lot of questions to be answered and it could take a while." Much longer than Hannah wanted.

The tears surged and she tried to hold them back.

"Oh, my baby. I want to be there with you. This was such a big day for you and—"

"Momma, Mr. Stevens is dead." Oh, why had she said that? She didn't need to tell her the gory details now. But it hurt so much, and she needed to confide in the woman who loved her most in the world. Unfortunately, the tears surged into a sob ready to burst out at any moment.

"Your boss? I'm so sorry." Momma gasped and choked. Holding back her sobs, too? "I'm worried about you. God knows, He knows your pain and my worries. He is there for you. Please don't forget."

It was so hard to believe God was here with

her at the moment, but she wouldn't disrespect her mother. Now wasn't the time to argue about faith. "I won't forget, Momma. I have to go now. I need to answer questions."

"I'll be praying for you."

"Thank you. I'll call again, but I'm not sure from what number."

"Okay, baby. Be safe."

Hannah ended the call as the voices outside the door grew louder. She could make out a few words. A man's angry voice.

"We need to question the witnesses as soon as possible. Before they forget something."

"And we needed to keep her safe."

Ayden.

But it wasn't Ayden who opened the door. Everly peeked in. "Hannah, Detective Mann is here to see you. Are you ready?"

She drew in a calming breath. "As I'll ever be."

Everly opened the door wider, and the detective stepped into the room. Thirtysomething, he was not at all what she expected, like she'd even given it much thought, but he was tall and athletic with piercing blue eyes and had a weathered look about him.

He gazed at her and it was like he'd taken all of her in with one look. He dipped his head in a nod. "I'm Detective Mann, Miss Kahn. I'd like to ask you a few questions."

She shrugged. "I understand."

"Hannah, I can stay with you." Everly's eyes were warm and compassionate.

"I'll be fine."

As she watched the woman step out of the room, she regretted her decision.

Detective Mann eased the edge of the sofa chair across from the coffee table that separated them, sitting instead of standing. To make her feel less intimidated? Well, it wasn't working.

"I know you've been through a traumatic event today." For some reason, his words sounded sincere. She wasn't sure what she'd expected, though she had never been questioned before. But maybe Judge Honor's conversation with her nine years ago had felt more like an inquisition and had colored her expectations.

Detective Mann dragged out a paper pad and pen and leaned back, with almost a defeated look. The trauma of the day was clearly getting to him, too.

"Can you please tell me everything that you remember happening?" he asked.

She closed her eyes. Where did she even start? At the beginning was best. "I knew something was wrong when my boss introduced me to his hired bodyguard this morning."

Seeing Ayden had set off the warning signals in her head.

If only she'd listened to them.

Ayden waited with Everly in the hallway outside the small conference room where Hannah spoke with Detective Lincoln Mann. Lincoln was a connection and friend to their family. He was ethical with a good moral compass and could be trusted, but he'd wanted to interview them separately. Ayden had no idea what Hannah would say to the man. How would she portray Ayden's actions—heroic? Or otherwise? Still, he worried for her state of mind. Ached for her role in this to be over.

Except he knew it wasn't.

The door opened and Lincoln filled the doorway. "I'm done for now." He glanced back at Hannah and frowned.

She remained on the sofa, her face in her hands. Anger surged through Ayden, and he glared at the detective. He started forward but Lincoln held up his hand. "Just give her a minute," he said, in an almost whisper.

Everly passed between them and through the doorway. "Yeah, just give her a minute. I got this."

At least his sister had seemed to connect with

Hannah—under the worst of circumstances, of course.

Lincoln gestured for Ayden to follow him. A few feet down the hallway and away from the door, he said, "Anywhere that you and I can talk?"

"Sure. In my office." Ayden led the other man along the corridor to the left, and then into the space he'd claimed as his own. Multiple screens displayed various news broadcasts that covered the incident along with their particular spin on the story.

Ayden stood with Lincoln and stared at the screens for a few seconds. It would be easy to get caught up in the news and let it engulf him in anger and frustration. A knot grew in Ayden's throat as he remembered the events—most of which hadn't been caught on camera—that had happened a few hours ago. His legs shook a little, but he wouldn't let anyone know how scared he'd been for them all.

For Hannah…

He cleared his throat, drawing Lincoln's attention to his desk. "My gun is packaged there on the desk for you to take. You'll want to get ballistics. I'm sure I hit one of the shooters."

The detective frowned. "We don't have any of the three shooters in custody. No bodies, either. We're checking hospitals, of course. Thanks for offering this up. We'll keep the gun for when we do find a bullet and get it back to you as soon as we can."

"I appreciate it."

"You did good, by the way," Lincoln said, studying Ayden. "Protecting her. And others."

That knot grew bigger. Lincoln said nothing about Stevens, whom Ayden had actually been hired to protect. Guilt lodged in his throat.

He needed to sit down. But he would remain standing as long as Lincoln was standing. And the guy continued to study Ayden long and hard, to the point he felt uncomfortable.

Times like these he almost wished he'd followed in his father's footsteps and taken up the Judge's mantle.

"So let's talk," Lincoln said as if it was just another day.

"Okay. You want to sit down?" Ayden moved around his desk and sat on the other side.

By the look the other man gave him, he had the feeling he didn't like this setup and would have preferred to question Ayden at the scene or at the precinct.

But his captain had approved this setup—for today, that was.

"What's your take on what happened?" Lincoln asked, his pen and pad ready.

His take on things? What *had* Hannah said?

He scraped a hand over his face, and started at the very beginning—

"Someone shouted 'bomb' and all chaos broke out."

Lincoln took notes as Ayden filled him in, providing more details than the man might have been accustomed to. Ayden had been trained to capture and record in his mind even the smallest of details.

When Ayden had finished, he waited for Lincoln to ask questions about his story, if he had any. Lincoln read through the notes. "Miss Kahn is fortunate that you were there to protect her. But she was under the impression that you had only been hired to protect Mr. Stevens. Is that correct?"

Here it comes.

"That's correct. But of course, my protection extended to anyone in need of help. Under the circumstances, I focused on Hannah after Stevens died."

"Because…?"

"I think that would be obvious. She's a natural extension of her boss."

"Anything more than that?"

What was he getting at? "She could have been targeted, too."

"Explain."

"A few rounds hit the wall near her head."

Lincoln's frown deepened. "Are you sure?"

After all the details he'd already given, the guy had to ask? "One hundred percent."

"She didn't seem as sure. But I understand that it all happened so fast."

"She isn't trained to capture the details, especially in these sorts of experiences," Ayden reminded him.

"Do you think Stevens was the primary target?"

"I don't have enough information to answer that."

"Okay, let's back up. Miss Kahn said she first became worried when her boss introduced his new bodyguard." Lincoln looked up from his notes and stared at Ayden.

Ayden stared back. He couldn't comment on her emotions, her assessments.

The detective arched a brow. "Do you have any thoughts on that?"

"No."

"Tell me about the circumstances under which he hired you."

"I was hired quickly and began right away, trusting Stevens that he only wanted me there as a precaution. He implied that he might get rushed by reporters. I was more of a deterrent."

My mistake. He stopped himself from fisting his hands that would give away the depth of his frustration. Part of his previous experience included threat analysis. Yep. He hadn't done the work like he should have and made the mistake of trusting his client. By the time he was at the office and got that overwhelming gut feeling that something was off, it was too late.

"And you didn't suspect that there was more going on?"

Yes. Yes, he had. And right now, he was mentally kicking himself. "Stevens would still be alive if he'd stayed with me."

"How can you know that?"

"I would have protected him with my life."

"It's true," the soft, familiar voice spoke through a crack in the door. Hannah stepped all the way in. "Ayden used his own body as a shield. I thought the same thing. If my boss had stayed with us, he would still be alive."

And Hannah might have been the one to die. Ayden felt like the blood had drained from his head to his feet at the thought.

Lincoln scratched his chin. "We'll need to figure out if there's a connection with today's activities—if Stevens was the target or if his death was collateral damage."

"Wait. What else happened? Was someone else killed? Something stolen? What am I missing?" Ayden asked. Probably plenty since he was not part of the investigation.

Lincoln rose. "Let me do my job, Honor, and I'll let you do yours." Again, he arched that annoying brow.

Stevens was dead. Ayden had failed.

He hadn't offered up his opinion, and kept to the facts, but now he would have his say. "What if someone wanted to create chaos so that Stevens could be killed? He was the target, but the chaos is confusing the investigation and could lead you in the wrong direction. He hired me for a reason. He suspected something. Feared something. He just didn't tell me everything I needed to know to prevent this from happening."

And that would never happen again. He couldn't afford it. He wouldn't *allow* it.

"I appreciate your input," Lincoln said. "If you think of anything else that could help, please give me a call." He handed off his card. "That's my cell."

They already had his number, but Ayden took the card as Lincoln lifted Ayden's packaged gun and excused himself.

Brett joined the detective in the hallway and started up a conversation as he led Lincoln away. Connections. Networking. Keeping those lines of communication open.

Would they frequently face these kinds of scenarios where law enforcement questioned them if he got this business off the ground?

His business.

Right.

The only business left at the moment was to protect Hannah until they were certain she was no longer in danger. But he had a feeling she wasn't going to so easily allow him into her life.

Though Hannah had entered his office, she'd said nothing after her words to Lincoln. The volume on the monitors had been turned down, but the images were still riveting. And tossed him right back to the scene. He could only imagine what they were doing to Hannah. He wanted to step closer. To take her in his arms. Ask if she was all right.

Instead, he shut the monitors off.

She needed to stay here at their facilities until they knew she was safe and no longer targeted.

"Ayden..." A tremble threaded her voice. "I need to get home to my mother now."

Right. He should have seen that coming.

FOUR

Hannah's knees shook, but she had to stand her ground. She could tell by that look on Ayden's face that he didn't like the idea.

His jaw worked as he measured his words.

He couldn't keep her here against her will, but still…she wanted his agreement. Why it was so important, she didn't know. Maybe she *did* know, but it shouldn't matter if he agreed. "You don't understand. Momma needs me. And besides…you can't make me stay here." She hadn't meant to say the words, but now that she had, she turned to walk out. She would have kept going, too, but he caught her wrist.

Whirled her around to face him. Those piercing eyes. Dark mesmerizing pools of concern that she'd often gotten lost in.

"Listen to me." He almost sounded desperate. "You could still be in danger."

"Come on. They were after my boss, not me. You don't know that anyone targeted me."

He released her wrist, and she took one step back, feeling like they were dancing all over again, only there was nothing at all romantic about this. With her increased pulse, she might be trying to fool herself on that.

He took a step forward, moving closer. Yep. The dance. Warning signals cascaded up her spine. Warning signals and pleasant tingles—this guy, she thought she'd gotten over him. "Thank you, though. For what you did back there. Thank you for trying to save him. Regardless of what happened to Mr. Stevens, you protected me, and for that I'm grateful."

He angled his head, confusion surging in his eyes as he continued to work that strong jaw. "Why don't you stay here then? Just until we know it's safe."

"Ayden, the city is crawling with cops. I'm exhausted and Momma is worried. Please…just take me home." Hannah didn't want to admit she was scared, but she knew once she got home, she would feel better and maybe think a lot clearer.

Like Momma had said, God was with her. She had to believe that no matter the circumstances, God was *always* with her.

His expression softened. "Okay. Maybe you can get some rest. It's been a long day."

And just like that, he gave in so fast that it surprised her, but she didn't have the clarity of mind to think on it. She let herself fall into an exhausted daze, trusting him completely as he ushered her out to the parking garage, then opened the door to a big white Suburban with black trim all around. Intimidating to complement the owner. Someone must have retrieved it for him from the Greenco offices where he would have parked earlier in the day. They'd ridden together over to the hotel.

Ayden steered out of the parking garage, through the security gate and headed out.

"You know, now that I think about it, I could just call an Uber ride. Or you could take me back to my own vehicle. It's still parked at Greenco." After she spoke the words, she realized how stupid they sounded—especially if Ayden was right and she was still in danger. She'd tried to convince him otherwise, because right now she didn't know what to think. All she knew was that she needed to get to her mother.

"I'll drop you off at your house, and then we'll secure your vehicle and bring it by the house later."

Why? So they could make sure it didn't have trackers on it, too? But she didn't ask. She didn't want to think about any of it. As he steered through the West Ridge toward the Tacoma metroplex area, she thought back to their past.

She'd never invited him to her home—back

when they had been dating. She'd been young and stupid. Okay, that was only a few years ago, but she'd been embarrassed, that the well-to-do son of a special agent and a judge might look down on her because of where she lived. And she hadn't wanted to plant seeds of doubt in his mind. She hadn't wanted to risk losing him once he found out about her life and how she'd grown up. Shame flooded her.

Oh, Momma.

And now, moving was out of the question. It would just take too much out of her mother. She stared out the window as they rode in silence for much of the way.

"Hannah."

His voice pulled her from her thoughts. "What?"

"Even though I'm dropping you off at your house, we're not done yet."

We're not done as in Hannah and Ayden? Or as in this predicament? Or maybe both. "What do you mean?"

"Maybe I can't convince you that you could still be in danger—"

"And even if I was, I haven't hired you to protect me, Ayden. So really there's nothing you can do."

She hadn't meant to sound so harsh. But the sooner they went their separate ways, the better.

If she needed protection, she could hire someone else.

Couldn't she?

She rubbed her shoulders and stared out the window—Mt. Rainier loomed in the distance. No matter they'd driven half an hour—it still stood like a sentinel over the entire region. She couldn't often see it because of the low-hanging clouds. But when the day was clear, the mountain seemed to take up the sky.

And that's a little how she felt about Ayden right now. When he was around, he took up all the space. All the oxygen.

And Hannah needed to breathe.

She needed her own space, and time, frankly. Time to process everything.

Ayden drove right by her house.

"Hey, you passed it."

"On purpose."

"Ayden Honor. Stop this vehicle right now! I need to get home. Need to see that my mother is okay. I need—"

"Relax. I'm just making sure no one is hanging out and waiting for you to get home so they can harm you. Is that okay with you?"

"Yes and no."

"You're going to have to explain that one," he said.

"I mean, yes, thank you. I appreciate that. On the other hand, I didn't hire you to protect me."

He quirked a brow. "You've changed. You used to be more decisive than this."

"I think I'm being pretty decisive." But she knew to what he'd been referring. She'd been decisive when she'd broken things off with him.

He slowed at her house and parked at the curb. The structure issues had been corrected and she was still paying off those loans, but Mom's illness and those medical bills had taken all the rest of the money. If she had the money, time and energy she would get out there and paint the house. However, life had thrown too many punches at her in the past few years, and as they sat in the car and looked at the house where she grew up, guilt weighed on her. That old familiar cringe of feeling less-than, of feeling like she couldn't measure up because she lived in a tattered home in the poor part of town, washed over her once again.

She readied to open the door, but he locked it. And she couldn't unlock it.

She turned to face him as he shifted to look at her. "You think you have to *hire* me in order for me to protect you?"

She stared at him, feeling incredulity rising. Could she not get rid of this guy? The thing was, she wasn't exactly sure she wanted to get rid of him. But that wasn't right, either—

He'd been correct about her indecision.

Why was he pressing deeper into her life? It felt more like he was forcing the issue, using her safety as an excuse. But it was a valid reason. And he was scared for her.

She clearly didn't want protection, let alone anything else from him. Scraping a hand down his face, he sighed. Sitting so near Hannah in the vehicle reminded him of old times. Her soft smile, gentle kisses, her hands around his neck. Those memories were in danger of being overshadowed by today's events. What was he thinking? They had *already* been overshadowed by the events of nine years ago when she abruptly ended their relationship the day he planned to propose. He'd seen the love in her eyes. They had talked of their future together. What had gone wrong? He needed fresh air and unlocked the doors. Shoving his driver's door open, he glanced at her. "Come on, I'll walk you to the house."

"You don't have to do that."

She got out before he did and seemed to take all the oxygen with her as she slid out of his vehicle, leaving it cold and empty where she'd been.

Get with the program, Ayden.

He hopped out and hurriedly followed her up the sidewalk. She'd hurt him all those years ago, and while he owed her nothing, he wouldn't leave her to fend for herself even if she foolishly turned him away. Like he'd told her, he was going to watch out for her whether she wanted him to or not. If something happened because he wasn't there, then her life was on him. But that could go both ways. He could try to protect her and fail, like he'd done with Stevens, and then her blood would be on his hands that way, too.

She was making this harder than it had to be. Usually, effectively guarding someone meant their cooperation.

She neared the door, and he quickened his pace so he could reach her before she left him out in the cold, though he had no idea what he would say to her once he caught up.

But he didn't have to worry. The door flew open before Hannah reached it. A woman in her midfifties, shorter than Hannah and with similar beautiful green eyes and facial features, hung on the door frame as if it kept her standing. She looked decidedly unwell, and not the kind of unwell that occurred when someone was worried or stressed.

Sick. Hannah had mentioned her mother was sick.

Her features were pale beneath what he suspected was a perfectly groomed wig, but her joy at seeing her daughter was unmistakable, and Hannah flew into her mother's arms.

Okay, now he should just go. He was intruding. Just before he pivoted to head back to his vehicle, her mother broke free.

"You… You saved my Hannah." Tears choked her voice. "Come on in."

How did she know?

Hannah shot him a warning look, but he wasn't going to tell her mother no. Ayden entered the small home and, though it wasn't fancy, he could feel the love. His parents' home had been professionally decorated, but now that he thought about it—it had also been cold and sterile. Both had been workaholics and they weren't often home. They expected their kids to be overachievers too.

He suddenly got the sense he was missing something in his own family.

"I'm Susan Kahn, Hannah's mother. Please call me Susan."

"Ayden Honor. It's good to finally meet you."

Susan flicked her gaze to Hannah and then back. "To *finally* meet me. Should I know you?"

Both anger and hurt flashed in the older woman's gaze.

"Um…" Hannah hadn't even told her mother

about him? An ache stabbed through him, just when he thought he couldn't be hurt anymore.

Ayden ran his hands through his hair and schooled his features, not wanting her mother to see his shock or add to the awkward moment.

"It's been a long day," he said. "It's good to finally meet you after this *long day.*"

Appreciation for his quick thinking, his save, swam in Hannah's eyes. For an instant, he felt the pleasure of having made her happy. Then reminded himself…

I don't care.

"Would you like to sit and chat?" her mother asked. "Cookies and coffee?"

"No, thank you. I should really be getting back." He said the words, though he had no plans to go too far beyond the house. He'd stick close enough to watch the place and see if anyone decided to come after Hannah.

God, please let it not be so. But after today, Ayden didn't think he'd been wrong in his assessment, nor would he take the risk.

"Okay, well, then, thank you for protecting my baby."

"Anytime, ma'am." *Anytime?* What kind of response was that? "I'll just see myself out."

He glanced at Hannah and then tore his gaze away. It landed on the plaque over the door with the words "The name of the LORD is a strong tower: the righteous runneth into it and is safe. Proverbs 18:10."

The scripture pinged through his heart. God was watching out for her, so Ayden wasn't alone in that. He appreciated the reminder.

Time to get out of here.

He stepped onto the front porch and fisted his hands, fighting the ache coursing through him. Then sucked in a breath.

Time to man up. He wouldn't let the past prevent him from protecting Hannah, especially when he'd failed to protect her boss.

Outside, he veered from the sidewalk. He would look around the house, check the perimeter, quickly, before her mother had a chance to notice. Moving around the side of the house he took in all the details of the neighborhood, and the backyard, fenced in, but the gate wasn't locked. An open invitation to a dangerous predator.

He stood off to the side in the backyard, and hoped to quickly take it in and then get out of there. The telltale sound of the door opening gave him a heads-up that he wasn't alone. Uh-oh.

Hannah stepped out onto the back porch and stared across the yard at him. "What are you doing?"

"I told you I'm protecting you." He walked the perimeter of the dilapidated privacy fence.

She glanced behind her and lowered her voice. "Momma's taking a nap. She's worn-out. The worry could have killed her. She's weak and isn't doing well." Hannah shook her head as if fighting tears.

He heard the defeated pain in her voice. What she wasn't saying. Her mother was dying.

Compassion flooded him. He rushed forward, hopped up the steps then drew her into his arms. "Oh, Hannah."

She didn't resist, and in fact, pressed her face against her hands and then into his chest and cried.

A barrage of emotions flooded him, and he tried to steel himself against the feelings that left him aching, gasping for relief. Seeing her almost get killed today, watching the drama unfold, had nearly been the end of him. It was hard enough to comprehend what happened earlier or that Hannah was still in danger, but this... He had no clue how to comfort her.

Except just to be here like this. Standing here with her in his arms and letting her release her anguish. It was all he could offer. But he just couldn't let himself get in this deep. Get so personal.

Then again, could he blame her for the decision she'd made years ago? They were both young and inexperienced back then. Now they were older.

And wiser.

Which meant that Ayden should be fully capable of keeping his emotions in check when it came to Hannah. The good and the bad—he locked away for now.

He couldn't be more grateful that he would only need to protect her...

From a distance.

FIVE

Her grief spent, realization dawned, and she stepped back. She'd cried into her hands, but at some point, she'd gripped his shirt and wept, soaking his shoulder.

Oh…

And the smell of him. That musky, masculine scent. Like Hannah, he'd changed into another shirt, but she didn't think he'd had time to shower or clean up, and she smelled the turmoil of the day on him. Ayden…she remembered so well his masculine scent from before, and the smell tugged memories from the vault. Pleasant memories. All of them, except that last one, there, at the end. Her fault.

His father's fault.

He couldn't know.

Earlier today, she'd been operating in survival mode, living in terror and fear, and she hadn't thought about his scent, but now…

It was heady. Could overwhelm her, even in

the face of her grief, adding more grief on top of it, reminding her of what she'd given up. What she'd lost.

But he was watching her with those dark eyes, taking her in. What was he thinking? She couldn't bear it. But she looked at his shirt again. Damp where she'd cried. Some of her traitorous mascara on his shirt, too. Oh, she had to look worse now.

She stepped back. "I'm so sorry, Ayden. I didn't mean to—"

"Don't." He grabbed both hands in his and held them gently. She could feel the strength and reassurance in his grip. "It's okay. I'm so sorry, Hannah, about your mother."

"You didn't know. It's okay. There's no need for you to be sorry or worry about us." Because yes, there it was, a new worry emerged in his eyes.

She pulled her hands free and took another step back.

Hurt rose in his gaze. "Why didn't you tell your mother about me?"

They had to do this now? Shame filled her. How did she explain? She couldn't take the hurt in his eyes and averted her gaze. "Ayden…why does it—"

"You're right. I shouldn't have asked. What happened before, your reasons for not telling your mother about me, none of it matters." The compassion disappeared in his eyes—the brown had turned dark and cold. She began to shiver.

Hannah recognized that he'd closed himself off for his own protection. That told her he was still emotionally connected. "Thank you for understanding."

Thank you for understanding? What did that even mean?

"Good night, Hannah." He hopped off the porch.

She watched him leave—he'd always been good-looking. Excited about life. But something in his eyes had shifted. Hardened. She worried she might have put that there, but then, no...he'd been through something in the last nine years that had put an edge on him.

Just before he made the gate, he turned. "Call me if you remember anything. Or...if you need anything."

Then he was gone.

But she suspected he wasn't *really* gone. He would be out there watching over her. That should make her feel better. Safe. She hated that she was even in a situation where danger could be lurking around every corner and waiting in every shadow.

But, Lord, why does it have to be Ayden watching out for me?

She crept back into the house, trying not to wake Momma.

But everything in her wanted to scream.

"Tell me…" Momma's pain-filled voice echoed from the corner.

"Oh, Momma, you startled me." Hannah turned to see her mother resting in the cushy love seat in the dark. The older woman had gotten up from bed. How long had she been sitting there, watching through the sliding glass door? Had she heard the conversation through the glass?

"Sit." Momma patted the small love seat in a reading nook they kept.

Uh… Hannah wasn't sure she was ready to talk about today, but she knew exactly what her mother wanted. "I thought you were resting."

"I can't. Not until I hear everything."

Hannah did as her mother asked and eased onto the sofa next to her then patted her thigh. Momma held her hand and leaned her head back against the sofa and closed her eyes. Today had drained her mother as if she'd been in the middle of the danger and chaos.

"I don't want to upset you," Hannah said.

"I'm already upset."

She blew out a breath. "I don't really want to talk about it. My head hurts."

Momma squeezed her hand.

"But Mr. Stevens is dead, and that's the worst

of all of this." Tears surged. "And I'm scared I won't have a job now. I was training to be his assistant. And he's gone. I know that sounds so selfish of me."

"No, baby. His troubles are over."

Maybe.

"I know…you're worried about how you will care for me if you don't have a job. How we will afford to live. Afford the insurance and everything it doesn't cover." Momma sighed. "If I could go back to work—"

"No, Momma. You worked all those years and took care of me after he left us. I'll figure it out. I'll make this work."

"Hannah, sweetheart, you have to give this to God. It's in His hands. I'm in His hands. You're in His hands. Pray, yes. Trust, yes. But do not worry for tomorrow."

Ah, Momma. Always handing out words of wisdom. Words from scripture. "I'm glad you have such strong faith, Momma." *Because one of us needs it.*

But Momma was right. And on top of all that they had going on, how would she give her mother the dream cruise they had been planning for so long?

"This Ayden Honor. What is he to you?"

"He's the man who saved me today."

"I mean more than that, Hannah. We tell each

other the truth, always, but you're keeping something from me."

Oh, boy. How did she tell her mother? How did she tell *Ayden*? Divulging the truth to her momma would deeply hurt her, when she didn't need that kind of pain. And sure, telling Ayden about why she'd broken things off maybe would have hurt him too, but the truth didn't matter anymore. They were not together.

"He's just someone I knew in college. An old friend. I haven't seen him in years." Hannah pushed from the sofa. "Can I get you anything? I… I want to go outside and get some fresh air."

"I'm fine right here. I'll rest. You get your air. Then when you're ready to tell me, I'll be waiting." Momma squeezed her hand, then let go. "I love you, my Hannah."

Momma wasn't having the half-truth Hannah had shared. Not trusting her voice, she simply kissed her mother on the cheek, then moved out into the backyard again. She sat on the porch steps and listened to the night sounds. Dogs barking. A television running too loudly nearby. A noisy cricket.

A person could make their plans but one thing—small or big—could change everything. And today, her life had been turned upside down. Someone else's decision had flipped everything on its head, and people had been hurt, killed, and now Momma could be hurt once she found out about who Ayden had been to Hannah, and why Hannah had hidden that.

Pain lanced through her. A familiar pain.

The same pain she felt that day she'd lost Ayden forever.

But she had much bigger concerns than the hurt she would cause her mother, if Ayden was right and Hannah was still in danger.

A knock at the window of his vehicle startled Ayden. He'd been sitting here for hours until eventually all the lights had turned out in Hannah's home except for a small dim light in one room.

That someone had startled him wasn't good.

He unlocked the doors and Brett climbed in. "Bro, Everly sent me to relieve you."

"I don't need to be relieved."

"Oh really? How about the fact that I surprised you? Dude, that should never happen."

He pressed his fingers against his temples. "You're right." *I'm off my game.*

"You haven't even showered since this morning. You protected people, saved Hannah, gave a statement. You're wiped. And add to that, there's this girl. You've got scrambled eggs for brains when you're around her. I never met her...you know, before, when you were crazy in love. But that's over now, right?"

"Can we talk about that another time? She could be targeted." He stared at the house shrouded in darkness, despite the one small light. At least a security light remained on two houses down the street, but it wasn't enough. He couldn't see in the shadows. The porch light had been turned off about 9:00 p.m.

"Get back to headquarters and get some rest," Brett said. "We'll regroup and talk about what we know in the morning."

"Have we heard anything?"

"Nothing more. Everly is digging into the dead CEO's background."

"You mean more than I did." Before taking that job.

If he hadn't been there today, what would have happened to Stevens? Hannah?

"Don't beat yourself up," Brett told him. "Let's get on top of this…though we're not getting paid. I like Caine's suggestion that we charge enough up front to cover the follow-through if it's needed."

"Good idea."

"I'm heading back to my car. I'm parked a block down. I'll drive closer as soon as you leave."

"It's not important to me that you're hidden.

I'd much prefer to deter anyone with bad intentions." Ayden peered at his brother. "Understood?"

"Understood."

"Let's try to get the police department to put a marked car out here. That would free us up."

"Agreed." Brett hopped out and Ayden watched his brother get into his own vehicle a block back while also watching the house.

Tension knotted his shoulders. Part of him wished he'd spot a guy stalking up to Hannah's home. Ayden would take him down and out and find out who was behind today's attack. He'd get rid of the bad guys and she would be safe to live her life.

Brett pulled up to the curb, parking between two houses. Ayden steered away and slowed at the stop sign, watching his rearview mirror.

He didn't go home, but instead headed up to the HPS facilities where he had a home away from home. In his living quarters, he cleaned up and changed into a T-shirt and sweats. He stared at the bed. No way would he be able to sleep, and besides, Everly and Caine were probably still up, too. It was for times like these, when they were in the thick of it, that he'd created live-in facilities so they could stay if they wanted. And he definitely planned to stay here and work through it.

If only Hannah had stayed, too...

Yeah, well, that might have come with a different set of problems. He scraped his hand down his face as he exited the room and headed to his office.

He entered his expansive workspace to find both Everly and Caine staring at the monitors.

He didn't engage as he headed to his desk and plopped in the chair. "What do we know?"

"Ayden." Everly's tone was even but held an edge. "Pull yourself together. We've been working contracts for two new clients while you were guarding Stevens. We're working on threat analysis for those as well."

"Stevens's death takes priority."

The day came crashing down on him.

After keeping his composure with Hannah, answering the detectives' questions, and then watching her house, this was the first moment he'd let his guard down.

And man, the pain stabbed through him.

He leaned forward and pressed his face into his hands.

"She's right, bro." Caine now. "Take a few moments and let it roll over you, but don't let it take you down."

Oh, Lord, am I in the wrong profession?

He drew in a calming breath. He would try wording it differently. "Yes, Stevens is dead, but let's not let his death be for nothing. Let's not let those responsible get away with it."

Ayden finally opened his eyes. "The police…"

"Will do what they do," Everly said. "And we'll do what we do and work together."

"She's right, Ayden. Our protection services must come with knowledge—advance knowledge regarding all the risk factors. Threat analysis. And in the case that we fail, we have to commit to follow-through to see where we went wrong."

"You and Everly decided this on your own, did you?"

"Not exactly," Caine said. "After what you said this afternoon, we all talked and decided you're right. We have to follow through."

Everly eased into the chair across the desk and rotated it halfway to glance at the monitors playing news feeds about today's incident. "And in this case, Hannah is involved. We're in this with you, Ayden. You're not alone. And Stevens's death is not on you."

Ayden stared at his siblings. He'd been afraid this dream of his was about to fall apart, and it still might, but at least he had his family with him. Those he cared about and loved were the perfect people for the job. "I thank God I have you. Both of you. Brett too."

"What can you tell me about Stevens that I don't already know?" his sister asked.

"He hired me to just show up and provide one layer of protection, or rather to be a deterrent to reporters or anyone who might insist on more answers." Strange, now that he considered it. Stevens wasn't the POTUS, but obviously he considered himself important.

"I know that. What else can you tell me?"

"He teased me with the idea that our continued services would be needed in the future regarding protection and…against potential espionage. Strategic planning against attacks as the company goes public."

Caine pursed his lips. "There's much more to learn about this situation."

"What I've learned so far," Everly said, "is that Stevens created cutting-edge geographic information system. GIS for short. GIS is a tech sector that looks to grow exponentially. Greenco focuses on environmental factors for designing cities along with more efficient clean water systems. The software is proprietary. Apparently population growth, water supplies, environmental risks—all of these are part of growing infrastructure issues." She released a breath. "I'm not sure if it was a coincidence or not that an environmental group was holding a conference at the same hotel during the incident. We can look into all angles, including competitors. Or someone who didn't want the system being used in their city."

Caine shrugged. "Honestly? It feels more like, dare I say it, terrorism."

"That's why I said *all* angles, so I'll ask Brett to keep a pulse on the investigation since he knows Lincoln pretty well, in case they learn something that tells us this wasn't about Stevens being specifically murdered. We'll look into this angle because we were hired to protect him, of course." And because Ayden believed Stevens was the target.

"And what about Hannah?" Everly asked.

"What about her?"

"What was she doing there?" Leave it to Everly to bring up the topic he wanted to pass over. "At twenty-seven, she's two years out from getting an MBA. Sharp and intuitive. She worked her way up starting—" Everly thrummed through pages on the edge of his desk. "Oh, right. By answering the phones. Boy, it had to cut her that she had to start at the bottom."

Ayden rubbed his temple. "Nothing unusual about that. Obviously once she got her foot in the door, someone saw her value."

Everly pushed from the chair and paced the room. "You're probably right."

"But something about her being there bugs you?" Ayden mused.

"Yes."

"It bugs me too, but I thought that I—"

"That because it's Hannah, you couldn't be sure." Everly leveled her gaze at him. "Your instincts have always been strong, Ayden, but they weren't good when it came to Hannah before. Still, don't discount your thoughts. Run them by us, your team. That's why we're here."

While her words were true to a point, Everly's constant jabs about Hannah were starting to grate on him.

Caine had his back to them, arms crossed, watching some of the more graphic footage taken by security cameras, passed on to them by Lincoln. Hannah hovered over Stevens, crying, some blood on her fingers and on her temple.

"Please, could you turn that off? I lived it. I can't take any more."

Caine flipped to a news station. "Hannah Kahn was his assistant. Could she be a target because of what she *might* know...as his trusted employee? Or what someone *thinks* she knows, but doesn't?"

"The possibility of either scenario is why we'll stick close to her, whether she wants our protection or not, until it's over," Ayden said.

Until it's over...

The words had such finality to them, and for some reason he didn't like them.

His cell rang repeatedly, the obnoxious ringtone pounding and vibrating on the side table. Ayden bolted upright in bed. He'd finally fallen asleep. He wiped his eyes and grabbed the cell, knowing it was Brett.

"What?"

"She left the house."

"What? When?"

"I saw a figure skulking around, and so I went to investigate. I spotted Hannah, sneaking around back. I followed her through the next yard to one street over where she caught an Uber ride."

Ayden glanced at his clock. "In the middle of the night?"

"Exactly."

"Please tell me you didn't lose her?"

"I'm tailing the driver now," Brett said. "I think she's heading to the Greenco offices, but I'll keep you updated."

"Don't do anything. Don't approach her. Wait for me."

SIX

The Uber driver dropped Hannah off at the Mt. Rainier Savings and Loans bank building where Greenco leased three of the fifteen floors. She paid and tipped the driver then readied to slide out of the back seat.

"It's kind of late." Rupert was a college student and had shared more than she cared to know about his life. "Do you want me to wait for you?"

"No, it's okay. I don't know how long I'll be. I'll call for another Uber."

He smiled. "Maybe it'll be me."

"Maybe." Hannah thanked him then got out and closed the door. She ran up the expansive steps to the glass doors. Locked.

She waved at the security guard behind the marble desk. He frowned but moved toward the door when he recognized her and unlocked it. "Miss Kahn?"

"You don't usually lock these doors at night, do you?"

"An extra precaution given what happened earlier today."

"Makes sense." She entered the foyer and headed for the elevators.

"Miss Kahn, I'll need you to sign in."

She hesitated. At least he hadn't tried to stop her. That would mean that Mr. Stevens's office hadn't been declared off-limits by investigators. She was Mr. Stevens's assistant, after all, and sure, he was dead now, but she shouldn't have to explain her reasons for going to the office in the middle of the night. No one was asking. *Yet*.

But she sensed that was about to change and if she was going to achieve her goal of gathering intel, it was now or never. That much she knew.

"Of course." She approached the desk and signed on the signature tablet. Melvyn, the night security guard, typed in her employee number as well. For a modern building, she had always been surprised they hadn't already employed biometrics of some kind.

Melvyn smiled. "Thanks, Miss Kahn."

"You're welcome." She hurried onto the elevator before he decided to ask her questions or remember that she'd been involved in today's incidents. Maybe he hadn't known. Her name hadn't been splashed across the news, and only those who knew her personally might have recognized her in the edited videos of the incident.

She pressed the button for the eleventh floor and inserted her key card for permission. Elevator music played softly. Even at night. Hmm.

Hannah hadn't been able to sleep and had tossed and turned. The exhaustion should have taken her, but all she could see was Mr. Stevens's body. His lifeless eyes. He'd had big plans today and death hadn't been on his to-do list. It often took people by surprise. The horror of it all... When she pushed her mind beyond the terrifying images she saw Ayden there, protecting her with his life.

So she couldn't sleep anymore and had to do *something*. She'd peered out her window and spotted a car—but Ayden wasn't sitting in it. One of his brothers. Caine or Brett, she couldn't be sure. She hadn't felt guilty about losing Ayden's brother as she slipped into all-black clothing and snuck through the neighborhood to meet the Uber driver.

In the car, she'd pulled a pink scarf out of her tote and wrapped it around her neck stylishly so it wouldn't appear like she was deliberately being clandestine.

The elevator door pinged open, snapping her back to the present, and she stepped into the posh yet environmentally friendly Greenco lobby. The beautiful caramel floors looked like wood but were actually bamboo. Everything in the office had been made from recycled materials.

And at the moment she didn't care. She only cared that the office was empty.

Behind her the elevator doors whooshed closed.

She crept across the foyer, her shoes squeaking on the polished bamboo floor, and once again she used her key card, to enter through the glass doors that remained locked at night. A few lights remained on so the place wasn't completely dark, but no one was working late, at least on this floor.

She suspected no one would want to come into work for a day or two after what happened today. But Hannah was on a mission to answer the question that had plagued her since this morning. One that Ayden also wanted to know.

Had she become a secondary target because of what she might know as Stevens's assistant? Even if she had, the bad guys had the wrong assistant. She didn't know all that much. Not yet. Nothing…worth killing for. But that didn't matter because if they thought she knew something, she was still in danger.

Hence another question—What did Stevens have going on that was worth murdering him over?

Hannah couldn't sit around and do nothing.

She pushed through the doors and walked

down the corridor on carpet made out of recycled pop bottles to her office that joined to his bigger one. She unlocked her door, then moved across to his office, unlocked it and then set her tote on his large executive desk. Mahogany. Not recycled material. She took in the panoramic view of the Puget Sound region to the west, and on the opposite end, Mt. Rainier was visible in the daytime.

Hannah sat in his chair.

It felt disrespectful.

What had been his last thoughts as he was dying? She breathed in deeply, holding the tears back. No time for that now. She had to learn what she could. She had more access to him than anyone, and yet, she didn't know what today was about.

Maybe at the end of it all, they would discover the shooting, the bomb threat, had been about the environmental conference instead. But she'd gotten the sense that Mr. Stevens had been pursued, and then her too, in the parking garage. If she waited too long, she would lose her access to his information.

Even Kristen, who had trained her to take her place before she went on maternity leave, had been locked out of the system as part of the company protocol. The information, the data, was highly sensitive.

And Hannah didn't understand it well enough to even know why. But she assumed proprietary software would always be held close, regardless of its purpose. Still, the way she understood it, Alfred's system merely organized and analyzed data and displayed it. It reduced expenses and improved operations, and in this case, helped create models for better infrastructure development, especially water systems.

But worth bomb threats? Murder?

Then again, what could Hannah know about how murderers and terrorists thought? Nothing. All she knew was that she'd liken them to psychopaths who had lost their ability to care about others.

At her boss's desk, she stared at his computer. She wasn't doing anything illegal. After all, the police didn't consider him a target, or they would have shut this all down as part of their investigation. They could eventually come to that conclusion and want to look at the office, the people and his computers, but Hannah had gotten here first and would get to the bottom of this.

If her life was in danger, then Momma's life was too, and she couldn't sit around and wait for someone to come and kill her, leaving her mother to be killed along with her, or left to grieve the loss and fend for herself through the rigors of battling cancer during her last days.

Hannah stared at Mr. Stevens's computer and booted it up.

Time to learn the truth.

He was going to get answers.

Maybe he'd had her all wrong.

Maybe she hadn't wanted protection because…

No. Ayden wouldn't let his mind go there. Except what kind of professional would he be if he didn't even entertain the thought that Hannah was part of it? That she was going into the office so soon after her boss's death disturbed him.

To the core.

Experience and training told him to suspect everyone, but he hadn't suspected Hannah. And his training would say someone on the inside should be suspected. And Hannah had been on the inside, and she was on the inside *now.*

His suspicions ramped up as he sped through the city toward the Greenco headquarters. Brett had already texted to confirm that she had in fact taken the Uber to the offices. Ayden had thought something had seemed off about her working for Stevens and now he realized he should have listened to his instincts. To the warning signals going off in his head that he'd ignored because it was *Hannah.* He'd thought the warnings had been related to their history together, and he hadn't wanted to be susceptible to her beauty and charm. The good person she was—but he'd been a fool.

In the past and in the present.

Still, he couldn't shake that the very idea of her being involved seemed preposterous. She had been in the line of fire today, so this kind of thinking didn't make much sense, either. But could she be an insider or informant working with whomever had targeted Stevens? After all, *he'd* been shot. Not her. Maybe the fact she had survived hadn't had one thing to do with Ayden's protection skills.

He swerved to a stop in front of the building. Brett emerged from the shadows where he'd been waiting just like Ayden had asked.

"I'm going up," Ayden said. "You wait here in case there's trouble. Don't put yourself in the middle. Call for backup instead."

"Wait…you think…"

"I don't know what to think." The situation would prove to be a double-edged sword if he was trying to protect the person who was also responsible, though indirectly, for his client's murder.

The big glass doors were locked, preventing him entrance, and he gently knocked so he wouldn't cause more alarm than necessary. Though warning signals jolted through his every nerve ending.

God, please let me be jumping to conclusions about Hannah. The last thing he should do was to storm in and accuse her. That would get him nowhere.

The security guard at the desk frowned and moved forward. He spoke to Ayden through the glass.

"Can I help you?" His question was muffled.

The man was right to be concerned after the events that had killed Greenco's CEO. "I'm here for Hannah Kahn. I was hired as protection. I met you earlier."

The guard, Melvyn, remembered Ayden from yesterday and unlocked the door, his keys jangling. Ayden entered the quiet building lobby. "Thanks. I'm late. I was supposed to already be here to watch over her."

"She's upstairs, but you'll need to sign in first. I'll just call and let her know you're on your way."

Uh-oh. Ayden scratched his signature on the tablet.

The security guard had the phone to his ear, and Ayden heard it ringing. What would Hannah say? Would she deny him?

The guard's eyes widened as he looked at something happening behind Ayden. Glass shattered with the sound of gunfire. Ayden dove behind the counter then pulled the security guard down with him. The man had pulled his gun and thought to do his job, but this was an ambush.

Blood gushing, the security guard grabbed his shoulder and moaned in pain.

"We need to call. For…help." He gritted his teeth.

But they couldn't reach up for the phones.

"Use your radio if you can but keep it down."

Ayden had to focus on protecting them, so he wouldn't be making that call.

From behind the counter, he returned fire. Two masked men dressed in tactical gear, obviously hired gunmen, stormed into the building. Behind them another man came in—no mask. No fear. His gaze searched the lobby then zeroed in on the corner behind which were the only two people who could stand in their way. Ayden and the security guard.

Ayden peered around the counter again in time to see the man in charge gesture to his men to take tactical positions.

Melvyn was down and out, and Ayden would soon be overwhelmed. Before that happened, he had to stash the injured security guard somewhere safe, and to get up to the main floor and to Hannah before it was too late.

"I'll get you someplace to hide. Keep putting pressure on that wound. Then I need to get upstairs, okay?"

Sweat covering his face, Melvyn nodded. "You'll need this to get to that floor."

He flicked his gaze toward the key card pass sticking out of his pocket.

"Thanks, man." Ayden snatched it up. "Can you make it?"

The man's pain-filled eyes were wide. "I'll do my best."

Ayden shouldered him, then laid down gunfire to cover them as they ran deeper into the building, beyond the elevators. Bullets chased them, pinging off the walls while Ayden kept praying the gunshots would miss.

"There," Melvyn grunted. "The utility closet. There ain't nowhere else."

Ayden didn't like leaving the man, but he had no choice if he wanted to save Hannah.

"I'll be okay. It's just a graze," he said. "You go help Hannah."

"And you get on your radio and call for help, too."

He nodded and shut the door, lifting up a prayer for the security guard, Hannah and himself. His gun at the ready, he crept along the wall. Could he make it to the elevators? He heard nothing in the lobby, not even sirens in the distance.

The assailants had disappeared. Had they taken the elevators? They wouldn't be able to access Hannah's floor if they had—at least not without a key card.

He crept forward toward the stairwell and cracked the door open. Boots bounded up the stairs.

Oh, no!

They would still need a key card to open the door to the Greenco offices, but if they didn't have one, he imagined they would blast their way through like they'd done at the building entrance. Ayden raced around the corner to the elevators, pressed the button and impatiently waited for the doors to open. He hoped he could get to the Greenco floor before the men. He was already behind—when he'd gotten here before them.

Frustration pulsed through him along with adrenaline. The doors whooshed open, and he rushed in. Using the key card he selected the eleventh floor.

God, please let me get there before them. Please keep Hannah safe.

SEVEN

Though she'd booted up the computer, she didn't know what she was looking for. She only knew that she had limited time to find whatever it was.

Lord, please guide me. Help me find the truth behind Mr. Stevens's murder.

The silent prayer seemed ridiculous—she wasn't an investigator, so what was she doing here? Yes, she was Alfred's "clone" assistant, but he was gone. And even though she had the *right* to be here, and she wasn't committing a crime, this…felt wrong. On the other hand, the police weren't here digging around in his files. She had the strong feeling that the answers to her questions might disappear, and she would never find the truth. The police would never find it, either.

Hannah only ever wanted to be above board. To do what was right in God's eyes.

And now, she had two things she felt wrong about on her internal radar. The first—cashing that check. But Momma had been on the verge of losing her house. The bank had sent the third notice and was about to start foreclosure.

And since Judge Honor hadn't actually had honor, Hannah had made a decision to use the money to pay off the mortgage. Removing that load of stress from their lives had been huge for her mother. Momma hadn't known about the check, only that the bank claimed that a mysterious benefactor had paid off the house.

Momma had thanked God.

But Hannah had kept the secret to herself and it had weighed heavy on her, eating away at her insides a little every day. And now here she was in Mr. Stevens's office, stepping near the edge of right and wrong once again.

The sickening thoughts swirled in her head, but she ignored the nausea. She had to do this.

She plugged the USB drive that would hold several terabytes of data and started transferring files, and while they transferred, she searched for a reason someone might want to kill her boss. A reason someone would want to kill *her*.

As she waited for the data to transfer, she pushed back from the desk.

Maybe she knew nothing before, but with these actions, she was certainly making a legitimate target out of herself. But she needed to find out what was really going on. Hannah had the gut feeling that if she didn't uncover the reasons now, they would be lost to the good guys.

Her cell rang and she stared at the caller.

Kristen?

The woman who had trained her to work under Mr. Stevens. Kristen, who clearly knew much more than Hannah. Had the woman had the uncanny thought that Hannah was in Mr. Stevens's office trying to learn the truth?

Should she answer? She'd have to steady her voice because right now she felt like a big bag of buzzing nerves.

She answered. "This is Hannah."

"Oh, Hannah. I'm so relieved to hear your voice! I…" Kristen sniffled.

She could tell Kristen couldn't speak due to her distress, so Hannah gave her a few moments to collect herself, then said, "Are you okay?"

The incident that left their boss dead had to put additional strain on the pregnant woman. Hannah wished she had thought to call her, but everything was happening so fast.

When she still said nothing through her tears, Hannah continued, "Kristen, you don't need this kind of stress. Maybe you should be resting."

"Don't worry about me. I'm fine."

"I'm glad to hear that," Hannah said. "But Mr. Stevens…" She couldn't bring herself to say the words.

"Listen." Kristen blew her nose. "I'm sorry to bother you. I know I called in the middle of the night, but I just had to hear your voice. I had to know if you were okay. I saw on the news what happened. I still can't believe it. I can't believe he's dead."

Hannah pressed her head into her crossed arms on the desk as she spoke into the cell. Eyes closed, she tried not to cry, too. "I can't, either."

"Where are you? I hope you're somewhere safe."

"I'm safe. Don't worry about me." Guilt flooded Hannah. But there was no need to involve Kristen or create more upheaval for her.

"How are you feeling? Everything okay with the baby?" Hannah had never met the father, and Kristen hadn't brought her personal life to work with her, so it felt weird even asking this simple question. But she knew that Kristen's due date was in a few short weeks.

"Being on bed rest is no fun but the baby is kicking me hard these days. I don't know whether to laugh or cry… Well, scratch that. Right now, I'm crying."

"For your baby's sake, please put your mind on something else." Who was Hannah to be giving advice?

"I promise, I'll try," Kristen said. "But it will help if you call me tomorrow or the next day, whenever you feel up to it and tell me what happened. It's late, and I shouldn't have called. I think I need to crash. But please…call me. Knowing what happened would help ease my worries."

Images flooded her mind again. She didn't want them, and Kristen didn't need them. "I'm not sure how much I can say since this is all part of a police investigation." Though she hadn't been warned away from speaking to anyone by the detective, holding the information close felt right, especially from Kristen, who didn't need more emotional stress.

"I will. I'll call as soon as I can. Um…" Should she even ask? But she needed to know. "Do you have any idea why someone would want to kill Mr. Stevens?"

A loud gasp sounded over the cell. "What… Hannah…what are you saying? You can't really think someone intentionally wanted to kill him. Is that what the police think?"

Oh, why had she opened her big mouth? But she had, and now she would try to repair the damage she'd done.

"I don't know what they think. I'm sure they'll get to the bottom of it. But for me personally, I just want to be prepared for that possibility. I'm wondering why it happened. Why was he killed today? Was there something he was hiding?"

Inwardly she groaned. What happened to her resolve not to talk to Kristen about what happened?

"I can't believe someone would want him dead, much less stage what happened at the hotel. I don't know what's going on. But Hannah...you should be careful. If someone was after Mr. Stevens, you could be in danger, too."

"Did you know he hired a bodyguard?"

Silence resounded for a few breaths. "No. I'm not there, so I wouldn't know. I considered staying in touch since I've had to take maternity leave before the baby's even born, but I trained you well, Hannah. The news said Alfred died in the chaos, and they mentioned nothing at all about him being murdered. The implication was that he was collateral damage during a domestic terrorist attack. But it sounds like...that's not what happened. What do *you* think?"

"I'm not sure what to think." Maybe someone didn't want the truth to come out, at least not yet.

"Well, I know more than when I called, but I... Call me soon and update me on everything."

"Sure. Please take care of yourself, Kristen, and be glad you were at home safe, preparing for your baby's arrival."

Kristen sniffled again. "Please—"

The line went dead.

Confused, Hannah stared at her cell. The call had dropped. In fact, she had no bars whatsoever.

She lifted the landline handset. No dial tone.

What was happening?

Her heart pounded. She bolted from the chair and moved to the window to look out. Down in the street, she saw… Wait. It looked like lights flashed. Police vehicles were approaching.

Fear squeezed her throat. What was going on?

She had a feeling she knew. But…it was surreal.

A noise sounded in the quiet.

A pounding noise. Someone beating on the door. Then a gunshot. Someone was trying to break into the locked Greenco offices. They must have gotten a keycard to even get to the floor, but regardless, she had no protection. No one here to help her. Now she realized what a huge mistake she'd made—Ayden wouldn't have let her come here.

Hannah yelped.

Hide. She had to hide.

She ran a circle in Mr. Stevens's office searching, but there was no place she wouldn't be found. She'd have to go on the offensive as a way of defense. Footsteps sounded on the bamboo floor. She moved to the wall behind the open door and lifted a big vase. It was heavy, but it would do, as long as she could lift it over her head.

Muscles straining, she lifted the vase and waited for the right moment, if it would ever come. But she had the feeling that moment was fast approaching.

A man rushed into the room, his weapon drawn.

She used the weight of the vase, allowing it to crash down on him even as he shouted her name—"Hannah!"

But it was too late. The vase cracked on his head, and he crumbled to the floor.

Ayden.

"Oh, Ayden!"

The voice broke through his daze as he struggled to scramble onto his knees. To. Get. Up.

Ignoring the pain lancing across his head and neck, he angled enough to peer at her, and croak out the urgent words, "They're coming. We… Have…to move."

"I'm so sorry I hit you over the head I didn't mean to I thought you were someone coming to shoot me." The panicked words spilled from her in one long sentence before she even dragged in a breath.

"Hannah. Calm down." He finally stood up and leaned against the wall to steady himself while the dizziness passed. "Let's go. We have to get out of here."

"But you're hurt, aren't you?"

"Mostly my ego." Okay. Yes, his head hurt. But he had only been stunned. And he was still alive. That counted for something. And he wanted to *stay* alive. "You caught me off guard and that should never happen." But like Everly kept telling him, being around Hannah distracted him.

"Your shoulder, too."

"What?" He glanced to where she pointed. His shirt was torn and a small gash oozed blood. "I'll live."

But he wasn't sure she would if he didn't get her out of here. Though he wanted an explanation as to why she'd come here in the middle of the night, and without the protection of a bodyguard, he could wait until she was safe to learn her reasons. But they had better be good. He'd wondered about her being an insider and accomplice to the attack at the hotel but given the way the armed men had crashed through the bank building on their way up, that had left no doubt that Hannah was a target.

But why all the firepower? Why the guerrilla warfare tactics? Did the men after her think she had the power or ability to mow them down with a machine gun?

She grabbed her cell off the desk. "The phones are down, and I can't use my cell. We can't call for help. But I saw police cruisers racing down the street. I hope they're here."

"I hope so, too. Maybe the security guard downstairs was able to call for help on his radio. I doubt the police can help us much since we're up here. They won't be able to make it in time. But I always have a backup plan."

Her eyes widened as he ushered her out the door. The men should be here any moment, and he was surprised they were not already upon them. His backup plan had *better* work. Hannah kept up with him, then suddenly stopped, tugging him back. He almost yanked her forward.

"Wait! I can't go yet." She pulled her hand free and then dashed back toward the office.

The elevator dinged.

Confusion slammed him. He'd been expecting them to hit the stairwell exit and break through there.

Before those doors could open, he had to get her out of here. They would not be taking the elevators.

"There's no time!" He grabbed her by the waist and hauled her through the exit and into the stairwell.

Just in time.

Bullets flew. Gunfire dinged against the door

and into the stairwell, banging the rails. Hannah kicked and screamed on his shoulder as he carried her, firing his gun to cover their escape.

"Put me down!"

"You're not going back in there," he muttered.

"I get that now."

Oh. Right. He set her down and together they continued running up the stairs. Stairwells and corridors. Again. This was like déjà vu.

Behind him, Hannah gasped for breath. "Where are we going?"

"The top floor." The building had fifteen. "Only one more floor to go."

"What? Why? We'll be trapped!"

"Trust me."

At the exit onto the building's roof, he waited for her to catch up.

Bullets hit the wall. Those thugs were still following. He shoved through, tugging her with him, then slammed the door closed and found a pipe, which he thrust through the locking mechanism.

On the roof, cold wind whipped around them, despite the summer season.

"Now what?" Her eyes were lasers shooting anger and pain. "We're trapped, just like I told you."

He eyed the door. The men were still trying to break through the steel door. The sound of bullets pinging against it resounded. Eventually, they would break through. And he'd better be ready.

"I got you out of trouble again, Hannah. Those men were going to kill you. You'd be dead right now if…"

"If you *what*? Hadn't followed me?"

"That's right. You snuck out of your house to get away from me." Ayden fisted and refisted his hands. He needed to get a hold of his emotions. Gripping his weapon, ready to protect her, he eyed the door then glanced at the night sky.

"Not you, your brother. But… I… You're right. I didn't want you, or anyone, to follow me."

"What are you hiding, Hannah?" he asked, wishing he could bite back the accusing tone that escaped.

"Nothing. I'm not hiding anything."

Whop, whop, whop…

The sound drew Ayden's gaze up, but he didn't miss the surprise on Hannah's face. "I hope that's for us."

Heart pounding, he prayed it was, too. Then he spotted Brett…

"Yes. My backup plan. Brett followed you here and I entered the building to follow you up when the men showed up locked and loaded, as if they were facing an army instead of one female assistant."

"So he called for a helicopter?"

"He secured it to fly it, yes." He grinned. "Company protocol. When bad guys are chasing you up a stairwell, escape from the rooftop."

The smile she sent him shot a warm arrow through his heart.

EIGHT

Inside the helicopter, Hannah donned a headset so she could hear conversation. But she didn't feel like talking, and frankly there wasn't much conversation going on. Tension filled the air inside the cab as the helicopter vibrated her whole body all the way to her bones.

Oh, wait. That wasn't the helicopter.

It was *her.*

She was shaking. Her hands and her legs. Her insides. Her teeth chattered. She was losing control.

"Hannah!"

Suddenly Ayden had turned to her and grabbed her hands. He forced her to look into his warm brown eyes. "Hannah…look at me…breathe. Just breathe."

Concern rippled across his features as he motioned for her to breathe in and out slowly, to model his actions. And she did. Maybe she was in shock after what had happened. But today hadn't been nearly as terrifying as yesterday. Was it a delayed response to the danger, or a cumulative load?

Maybe it was just all too much.

"Hannah? Hannah…listen…"

His words finally pulled her back and she focused on Ayden. His strong jaw. Kind brown eyes. Thick, dark hair…which she wanted to reach up and run her fingers through. She lifted a hand, but then lowered it again. What was she thinking? That was just it—she *wasn't* thinking.

"It's going to be okay," he said. His voice was steady and even and wrapped around her.

He was trying so hard to convince her.

"How can you say that? We know they're after me now. And I left the USB drive." She pressed her hand over her face. *How could I have left it?* And it was there now, for them to take. All that information exposed. She'd been a fool.

She dropped her hand to find him looking at her again, and that suspicion sparking behind his gaze. She hated that she'd given him a reason to be distrustful of her.

"What was on it?" Accusation edged his voice.

She didn't like his tone one bit. But she wasn't sure how she could put his fears to rest. She wasn't the bad guy here. That he for one second would suspect her involvement rankled. That was another reason why she could never tell him the true reasons she'd broken up with him all those years ago.

She turned to look away and think on how to explain what was on the USB when she didn't know yet. Explain why she'd downloaded data in the first place without giving Ayden more reason to doubt her.

The helicopter angled away from the building. She spotted three men on the rooftop. They'd apparently broken through the door.

Relief rushed through her. "I'm so glad you had a backup plan or else we'd still be on the roof and facing off with those guys. You must have a lot of resources."

"HPS has contracted with the county for helicopter use." He shrugged. "Now I know I was right to get everything in place just in case."

A buzzer went off somewhere up front, coming from the dashboard.

Her heart jumped to her throat. "What's that sound?"

"Brett?" Next to her Ayden stiffened. *"Brett!"*

Another sound reverberated through her. The helicopter… Something was wrong. "Ayden?" She locked eyes with him, and the uncertainty in his own gaze sent a wave of fear through her.

"I think they hit the tail," Brett said. "Hold tight, guys. I'm sorry. I'm afraid we're in for a hard landing."

"A hard landing? Ayden?" She grabbed his arm and squeezed so hard that he peeled her fingers away.

Ayden gently gripped her hand and held tight. She tried to soak up comfort and reassurance, but they were going to crash.

Oh, no! "A crash landing." She gasped. She sucked in a breath, but still felt like she was suffocating. She couldn't breathe. "Is that even survivable?"

"I'll do an autorotation," Brett said.

"What's that?"

"Landing without power, but it'll work in the case of tail rotor failure since there's virtually no torque. Just hold on. And pray."

"We'll be okay," Ayden promised.

Hannah didn't understand anything Brett said except for the *hold on and pray* part. And Ayden sounded as if he was trying to convince himself they would live.

I don't want to die. Not yet anyway. Her mother. What would Momma do if Hannah died? Hannah squeezed her eyes shut. "Let's pray. That's all we can do right. I hope my mother is praying for me. God listens to her."

Tears squeezed out around the corners and slipped down her face.

If she was ever going to tell Ayden about what happened, now was the time, wasn't it? But fear squeezed her throat and choked her. No words would come out.

Ayden prayed out loud, and listening to his confident voice vibrate through her body and her heart, she could almost believe they would survive. He squeezed her hand and she prayed along silently, the knowledge that he could turn to God right now warming her heart in all the right places.

His voice was shaky, and yet strong at the same time as he prayed for God's mercy and grace, for God's will and protection. He prayed for protection for her...

For *her*?

What about himself and for his brother?

The helicopter was spinning, rotating, going down, down, down. Nausea erupted—it was like the worst carnival ride ever because it was real.

This was real.

She gasped and sobbed. She opened her eyes because keeping them closed sent acid up her throat, made the nausea swirl even more in her stomach.

"Brace yourselves for impact!" Brett shouted, though he didn't need to shout through the communications.

The helicopter bounced and skidded. Metal twisted and crunched.

We're going to die!

Screaming. More screaming all around her. Hannah heard the incessant cries outside her body. But they were her *own* screams.

Darkness edged her vision.

"Hannah! Come on, wake up."

Her long auburn hair covered her face and he pushed it away. She moaned, then moments later, her big green eyes fluttered open, and she focused in on him, fear residing in her gaze.

Relief whooshed through him. She was coming to. Her lids fluttered again, and her big emerald eyes opened and stared right at him, nearly taking his breath away like the first time he'd seen her. But this situation was entirely different.

"Hurry!" Brett's shout snatched Ayden to the moment.

His brother hovered outside the fuselage of the crashed helicopter. Brett had done a fantastic job of landing—they'd survived, and the cabin was mostly intact.

"Okay. She's waking up. Let me just…"

A deep frown carved into her beautiful but stunned features. "Ayden. You're okay." Her words didn't go with the frown.

"Yes, I'm good. Now, let's get you out of here."

He suddenly realized that her expression probably had everything to do with her predicament. The pilot seat had crumpled back over her legs.

Panic engulfed him, and he couldn't catch his breath.

God, please don't let them be crushed. Oh, Hannah... He composed his features so he wouldn't give away his fear. "Are you in pain?"

She shook her head, but she could still be injured. "I'm going to shove the seat forward and I need you to pull your legs out."

If they weren't crushed. Trepidation slithered through him, but he would have faith. He had to believe she was okay.

"The tail is crumpled. Fuel is leaking," Brett shouted. "Get out. Now! This thing could blow."

Ayden held her gaze, willing her to trust him. "You ready?"

She nodded.

Digging his shoulder into the leather seat, he shoved forward, and up, trying to lift it. Gritting his teeth, he used all his strength, but it still wouldn't budge.

"A little help in here?" he shouted over his shoulder.

Brett crawled in behind him. "You're taking too...long."

Ayden didn't like the fearful tone in his brother's voice. But if nothing else, it speared urgency through him.

"Help me, Brett. Help me get this seat off her."

"But she could be—"

Injured. Paralyzed, even. Hadn't Brett just said they had to get her out before the helicopter blew up? "She's not. She's fine. Aren't you, Hannah?" He leveled his gaze on her. Saw the sweat beading at her temples. "Please tell me that you're good."

She nodded, vehemently, almost as if she could make it true by wishing it so. "I'm good. I don't feel any pain."

He shared a brief look with his sibling. Not feeling any pain could mean she was definitely injured and that it was preventing her from feeling anything at all. But she hadn't said that, and he was letting fear get the best of him. Besides, they didn't have a choice. There was no time to wait for an ambulance or the Jaws of Life to cut her out if the helicopter could be about to blow up.

"I'll go around to the other side," Brett said.

Precious moments ticked by. At any minute, the fuel could ignite and race up to the chopper's fuel tank and they would be toast. History.

He squeezed his eyes shut. *Lord, please protect us.*

Hannah whimpered.

He opened his eyes. "What is it? Are you okay? Are you hurt?"

"No. Just scared. Sorry."

Brett appeared at the door next to Hannah.

"I'm here. Let's move this seat." He eyed Ayden and nodded.

"Let's do it."

Together, they lifted the seat and shoved it forward. Ayden gritted his teeth against the strain. *Come on, come on, come on.*

"Hannah, you can do this, honey. Pull your legs out."

She groaned and tugged, lifting her knees. "I'm good. I'm out!"

Relief washed through him yet again. He and Brett eased the seat down, and Ayden scooped her up in his arms, then backed out of the helicopter. With her still cradled against his chest, he hurried away from the danger until he was at a safe distance. Brett stayed on his heels until he stopped. They turned to look at the helicopter. Anticipating a possible explosion, Ayden gasped for breath as he waited and watched the crashed bird. Wonder coursed through him that they had all three survived the crash.

Fire ignited then…an explosion resounded. Helicopter chunks, shrapnel, burst around them. Flames licked the sky. Even from a safe distance, he could feel the heat.

He took in their surroundings—a grassy knoll near an office complex next to the lake. They could have hurt others, had this happened in the middle of the day instead of the middle of the night. His throat grew tight and dry.

Thank You, Lord. Their lives had been spared three times tonight. The men after her, the crash and now the explosion. He just didn't know how much more they would have to endure. That *she* would have to endure.

"Um, Ayden...you can put me down now." Her voice was warm and soft against his cheek.

He'd been focused on the explosion and keeping her safe and releasing her had never entered his mind. She could have died too many times tonight. Could have been injured. Paralyzed. He didn't want to relinquish her and would rather hold her a little longer. He savored the way her soft form fit against him, the dizzying tingle triggered by her nearness, and suddenly the sweetest of memories rushed over him as he remembered all that he'd loved about Hannah.

And then he felt the sting of those memories. The painful bite.

A fire truck pulled onto the lawn along with an ambulance. Firemen jumped from the truck and hosed down the flames. EMTs burst from the ambulance and rushed toward them.

Ayden released Hannah and instructed a female medic to look her over.

Before he succumbed to his own examination, he pulled Brett aside. "You did good, bro.

Coming for us like that. And that landing…you saved our lives."

"I knew when I saw those men ambush the lobby and you were on your way to the top, I'd better head over per your protocols. Good call, man. And County had a helicopter parked on pad a couple of blocks over next to their headquarters, so that gave me a chance to get back fast as well as alert the locals." Brett had been a warrant officer, flying helicopters in the military. Tonight had been harrowing, but Ayden saw now what a great team he and his siblings made.

A long time ago he'd thought he and Hannah made a good team, too.

He sat on a gurney as a medic tended to a cut on his forehead, and stared across the space at Hannah as a medic urged her to lie down on a stretcher. They were taking her in. She could still have internal injuries.

On too many fronts…she wasn't out of danger yet.

NINE

Hannah shivered though the blue-haired medic named Lacy had placed a warm blanket over her in the ambulance. The paramedic had started an IV and explained Hannah was in mild shock. And here she'd felt silly being rushed to the hospital in an ambulance.

"You survived a helicopter crash, hon. That's something to be grateful for," Lacy said. "Count your many blessings as my grandmother would say."

"Brett landed the helicopter, but it was a hard landing." Maybe not a real crash, or they would be dead now.

I thought I was going to die.

"What about my friends? Are they okay?" Why was she asking? She'd seen both Brett and Ayden standing there, but also medics had been talking to them both.

"I think they're going to the hospital too, hon. We'll take good care of you. Your friends, too."

It was all she could hope for.

She shut her eyes to try to stop the flow of tears from spilling down her temples as she lay on the stretcher. The terror of the last several hours whirled in her head like a tornado, a vortex trying to suck her up and trap her forever. She pushed past those images and thought of Ayden... He'd been there at every single turn.

And whether she'd wanted him to be or not. She tried to tell herself he had to be a bad person too, somewhere deep down, because his father had been the worst sort of human. Someone who judged others, literally, and yet committed crimes behind the scenes, taking bribes to change the outcome of criminal trials. Ayden was his son, after all, and the apple didn't fall far from the tree—at least that's how the old saying went.

But that couldn't be true... Hannah's father had been the worst sort of person too, and Hannah was nothing like him.

When Ayden had held her close, she'd felt safe and cherished, though she knew that his actions had nothing at all to do with cherishing her. But...wow...she could totally have been fooled by the protective vibe emanating from him. And the tenderness.

She could have let herself linger in that feeling. For a few moments in his arms—despite the shock of the crash—she'd soaked up the emotions coming off him and wrapping around her. She could have stayed cocooned in his arms for an eternity. Or at least the rest of the night.

Being in his arms had the strange effect of reminding her how her father's presence conveyed the complete opposite of safety and protection, especially given the violence he'd shown toward her mother. It had taken a lot for Hannah to allow Ayden into her life, her heart, all those years ago, because she'd been conditioned to believe that men couldn't be trusted. She'd taken that risk with him and had almost been fooled when Ayden's father had proved her right.

Men couldn't be trusted.

At least she hadn't let Ayden all the way in. She'd never told him about her alcoholic abusive father. Never taken him to see her mother. Because she'd been embarrassed. Ayden's father had driven it home for her when he'd offered her a check to stay out of Ayden's life. The worst part—she'd taken it.

She'd been too stunned. She'd taken what he'd handed to her and held it as he explained what it meant.

Hannah recalled that moment she sat on the park bench, the judge walking away from her. She pressed the check that represented all the pain she'd felt her whole life against her chest, and cried, huge racking sobs. The judge hadn't thought her good enough for Ayden. In fact, she hadn't thought herself good enough either, but she could pretend at least for a while. And the man had shined the light on her secret truth—she came from a poor family and was the product of a worthless father, though he'd died long ago.

And she'd taken that check, broken up with Ayden as requested and lived with the shame of her actions every day since.

But the truth was, she'd been keeping secrets from Ayden long before the judge stepped between them.

And now, that was another big secret—the reason why she'd broken things off with him. She'd taken that check, at first, but then…she'd tried to give it back.

She could never tell him what had happened next.

So they could never be together. She shook her head—the confusing thoughts had no business in her mind when her life was constantly being threatened. But it was easier to think about troubles of the heart, the betrayals, than the psycho killers after her.

The ambulance suddenly stopped, and the doors opened. EMTs pulled the gurney out and pushed her through the emergency room entrance. Lacy bent over her and squeezed her hand. "You're in good hands now. Take care."

She watched the woman's face briefly as the stretcher was rolled away. Then she let the numbness set in and instead watched the ceiling tiles, tears still streaking down her temples and soaking the pillow.

Lord, what is happening to me?

Ayden marched down the sterile hallway following a nurse, the antiseptic scents accosting his nose. He hadn't needed an immediate examination and promised to check in with his personal doctors if he started feeling any pain. But since Hannah had experienced more trauma than he or his brother, they'd ordered tests to be sure she was okay. X-rays, and he wasn't sure what else.

Brett had waited to meet Caine and Everly in the waiting room and give them an update, while Ayden went in search of Hannah. He'd learned the security guard, Melvyn, was recovering from surgery to remove the bullet and was expected to make a full recovery.

Ayden was relieved to hear it.

Finally, the nurse paused at a door, glanced at him, then knocked. She poked her head through. "You have a visitor. Can we come in?"

"Yes," Hannah said. "I'm good."

The nurse opened the door and Ayden followed her inside the small room. She pulled the curtain along the track out of the way. Hannah was sitting on the examination table as if waiting to get out of here, expectation in her eyes.

"Thanks for coming to get me," she said.

He almost laughed. "Of course. I was already here. I'm in this with you." He glanced at the nurse, willing her to give them privacy.

"I'll be back with discharge instructions." She exited and closed the door behind her.

"What did the doctor say?" He looked her over, happy to see that she had good color in her cheeks.

"I'm fine. I could have bruising on my legs, but right now they feel fine. I can call my primary care physician if anything comes up. The ER doc's mostly concerned about back pain."

It was a hard landing, though, so they could all face that issue. Still, relief swelled inside. He took her hand, remembering the moment when he thought she might be seriously injured, or they might both have died if he hadn't gotten her out from under the seat before the helicopter exploded. They needed to have a serious talk about everything that happened tonight.

But not now. Not yet.

He had priorities and he hoped she was on the

same page. "Once you're released, we need to figure out where you're going next."

Her brows pinched together. "What are you talking about?"

"Your well-being, what else? You need to stay at a safe house until this is over. Surely you now realize that after what happened tonight. If you had any doubt before about being targeted, they should no longer exist."

"Going to a safe house isn't as easy as all that. I won't leave my mother. She's terminal and could only have a few months left. I will not go into hiding, afraid for my life, and leave her alone."

"Then will you put her life in jeopardy by staying with her and bringing that danger to her?" He took a step closer. "My suggestion includes your mother. She'll be at a safe house too. That way she's protected, and you don't have to worry." *God, please...let her see reason. Help me keep her safe.*

His gut clenched as he waited for her response.

Tears welled in her green eyes, and that sent a stab of pain through his heart, but they didn't spill over. More than anything, Ayden wanted to hold her again.

This woman broke your heart! Don't forget it.

The air in the small space grew stifling.

"My mother—" she hung her head as if grasping for the right words, then lifted her face "—she receives weekly infusions for her illness. It's not possible to *hide* somewhere. Don't you understand?"

Okay. Ayden hadn't even thought to ask about her medical treatments. He clasped his hands behind his back and closed his eyes for a moment to think.

This couldn't be the first time someone with significant health issues needed to stay in a secure place. He opened his eyes again. "Then we can figure out how to get a nurse to come to the safe house."

Still, that would also be a risk and could expose Hannah and her mother.

"Or we can transport your mom from the safe house to get her infusions. We'll figure it out. But the best solution to ensure your safety is to find out who was behind the attack at the conference center. Who was behind the attack on *you* tonight? It might help if you told me the truth. You never answered me about what was on the USB drive. Tell me what you were doing in Stevens's office."

She rubbed her arms and averted her gaze.

Suspicion curled through him. Hannah wasn't involved in the bad going on here. She couldn't be. And he couldn't feel this crazy suspicion about a woman he'd once wanted to marry. Had he not known her at all?

"Just like you," she said, "I simply wanted to know what my boss was up to. I was his assistant. His 'clone,' but I hadn't seen anything that would raise my suspicions. Maybe he hid something from even me. It was his company after all. He wanted me to see what he wanted me to see and nothing more. I thought if I could copy all his files, I could look through them to see what came up."

If Hannah was telling the truth—and he wanted to believe she was—then he was more than surprised that she would suddenly turn detective and want to investigate. She'd almost been killed, and her life was at stake, and yet she walked right back into a dangerous situation because she was determined to find the truth?

She was still hiding something, though, he could tell. And he wouldn't stop probing until she told him everything.

Including why she ended things with him.

If he just knew the reason, then maybe he could move on, even after nine years. Regardless, he knew better than to let himself feel anything for Hannah. He remembered the betrayal of the past and that should be enough, but something about this woman he once loved had enchanted him all over again. So he steeled himself against her captivating green eyes and concentrated on the matter at hand, like any good protection specialist should. One that didn't have a past with the woman he safeguarded.

"Why not wait for the police?"

"The police! Come on, they aren't even considering his death a murder. They think Alfred's death was just collateral damage."

He said nothing but just waited and listened. Maybe she would keep talking.

"And I was afraid that if he was killed for a reason, that reason could disappear."

"Disappear how?"

"Someone could destroy the files. Whoever was behind this could find them and make them disappear."

He crossed his arms and leaned against the wall. "I hope you realize that by doing this, you've made yourself even more of a target."

"You made it clear I was a target before. At least I was being proactive."

And then he felt it. That respect building, growing into glowing admiration, for her courageous actions in the face of unspeakable danger.

She'd been proactive all right. Going right into the proverbial lion's den—with gunmen storming the building after her, not caring who they killed in their path.

It would seem HPS hadn't been the only ones

watching her. With the thought, tension built in his shoulders. He rubbed his neck, unease vibrating through him.

Given the mayhem he'd witnessed over the last forty-eight hours, just sitting here in this ER could put people at risk. He grabbed her hand. "Come on, we're getting out of here."

"But I'm supposed to wait."

"We're not waiting around here for you to be targeted again."

Her eyes widened and her hand slid to her throat. "Someone else could die because of me."

Or you, Hannah. You could die.

TEN

Her chest remained tight, her breaths coming much too fast as Ayden led her out of the hospital and into the parking lot. He opened the door for her, and she slid into the back seat of Everly's silver SUV, the same vehicle that had picked her up after the bomb threat and the shooting. Except Caine was at the wheel this time.

Everly sat in the front passenger seat, her expression grim.

Ayden hopped into the back seat next to Hannah, but she couldn't look at him and instead stared out the window. She had caused all this, hadn't she? Hannah had crept out of the house, slipped away while Momma slept, and had planned to be in and out within a couple of hours. She would have been back in her bed and slept in a little, then made breakfast for her mother.

After all, she wouldn't be going into work just yet. The human resources department had to understand that Hannah needed a few days to re-group. Process everything. She should probably call someone tomorrow to see what was what.

As in, what was she supposed to do now that her boss, the founder, the brains behind the company, was dead? Was someone waiting in line to take his place? She didn't think so.

"Hannah."

She started at her name, then realized Ayden had been trying to get her attention, but she'd been lost in her own world.

"I need to get home," she said, without waiting on him to speak. "My mother has to be worried sick. I should call her but…better I just tell her in person."

"We're heading there now," Everly said, "but there's something you should know."

The way the woman spoke, the solemn tone in her voice, left no doubt that she was worried. A million scenarios ran through Hannah's head.

Her breath caught. "What? Has something happened?"

"Yes. It involves your mother."

Oh, Momma! She should have stayed with her mother. She should never have left. She clenched the armrest. "Tell me what's going on."

"The police have been called to your address."

"Wh-what do you mean?"

"We don't know," Everly said softly. "Brett

texted me the information. Dispatch received an emergency call from a neighbor regarding a break-in at your address. Brett is on his way there right now, too. The police are probably already there, so just try to calm down."

How was she supposed to *calm down*? This was her mother they were talking about. Hannah wanted to scream.

Instead she pressed her face into her palms and prayed.

Lord, oh, Lord, please keep my mother safe. I don't have her for very long on this earth. And I couldn't take the guilt if something I did brought danger to her. Please forgive me for my sins, my mistakes, and don't let harm come to my mother.

She believes in You. She trusts You...

Be her strong tower, like the scripture over the door.

When no more words would come in her silent prayer, she simply let her heart cry out to God.

Hannah rested her head against the seat back and kept her eyes closed, but tears streamed down again, and she couldn't stop them even if she wanted to. Because right now, she didn't care. No one spoke—no platitudes or lies or promises—for which she was grateful.

She sensed when the car slowed and stopped. Emergency lights flashed outside her home. She didn't wait for permission and flew out of the vehicle, racing to her family home. Shouts rang out behind her. Ayden and Everly, calling her name. Pulling her back.

But it wasn't their mother in danger and she paid them no heed.

She rushed up to a police officer. "Please, where's my mother?"

"Excuse me, ma'am, this is a crime scene, you'll have to—"

"A crime scene? This is my home! Where is my mother? Please tell me she's okay."

He stared down at her. "Just calm down. The medics are attending to her now."

Her eyes flicked to the open front door. Why had she even bothered to stop and ask? Hannah didn't wait for more information and dashed away from the law enforcement officer, again to shouts chasing her, though this time from the policeman. She raced through the small foyer, around the corner and into the hallway, then the bedroom.

Momma lay on a stretcher with an oxygen mask. Her eyes were closed.

Hannah rushed forward. Gasped. "Is she…is she…" Her mother was alive. She wouldn't be wearing an oxygen mask if she was dead.

Oh, thank You, Lord!

Her legs shook and she almost collapsed against the stretcher. A hand came around her waist and steadied her. Hannah thought to move away then realized it was Ayden.

The man in the medical uniform adjusted the oxygen mask. "Her vitals are stable."

Right. Not completely stable. She was on oxygen, after all. Her mother's eyes opened and found Hannah, then tears sprang from the woman's eyes. Hannah smiled with relief, her own tears joining Momma's as she grabbed her hand. "I'll go with you to the hospital."

Her mother shook her head.

Hannah glanced at the medic. "She's trying to talk. Is it okay to remove the mask for her to speak?"

"I can fill you in. She's refusing transport to the hospital. Claims there's nothing wrong. And in truth, as I said, her vitals are stable. She refused to go because she was waiting for you to come home. Said you were missing."

Her mother sat up on her elbows and tugged the mask off. "I'm not an invalid. You were gone. In the middle of the night, Hannah, you were gone. I was scared. With what happened, I thought you were kidnapped. I got up and tried to find the card, the number of your friend who's in protection services, when I heard a noise. I crept to the laundry room…and someone was breaking into the house!"

Her mother started gasping, and the medic secured her back on the pillow with the mask in place. "I really think she needs to be monitored, but at the hospital a doctor can make that call."

Hannah would love to know what happened next, but she suddenly realized the house had been torn apart—while her mother was inside—and terror ripped through her. She could find out the details later when her mother was calm. Hannah gritted her teeth. She'd been so focused on finding her mother and making sure she was all right, it hadn't registered that someone had trashed everything.

Why? But her mother was the priority right now. Material things didn't matter. They could be replaced.

To the medic, she nodded her agreement, as she spoke to her mother. "Let's make sure you're one hundred percent okay, Momma, and then you're going with me to a safe house."

She held Ayden's gaze as she said the last words.

He'd been right all along.

Ayden paced the hall outside of Hannah's mother's hospital room, frustration boiling through him.

Brett appeared at the end of the hallway and strode over to him, his expression unreadable, as usual. He leaned against the wall and crossed his arms, forcing Ayden to stop pacing if he wanted to hear what his brother had to say.

"Well?" He kept his voice low.

"We have two safe houses arranged. Two hotels. One for her mother, for now. We're still working out the logistics for the infusions. Apparently, it takes a whole new insurance authorization to get a nurse to come to her, so that's out."

"Understood. One of us can take her to get the infusion this week, and we hope and pray that by this time next week…"

"The bad guys will be put out of their misery, or rather, out of *our* misery."

"Yeah. Wouldn't that be great?" He frowned. "What do you think about the break-in at her mother's house?"

"You mean, who do I think is responsible?"

"Yes."

"What we've seen happen so far…this guy along with two goons…is a hired assassin. I say her mother is fortunate to be alive."

"You think the break-in was related to the same men."

Brett scratched his jaw. "A random break-in like that, right after you were attacked at the bank building? The chances are close to zero."

"So what, they tried to get to Hannah, and then shot the rotor out, and they must have seen the helicopter crash. Wouldn't they think we were dead?"

"They somehow learned you had survived. So they headed to the house. Maybe they thought to wait for Hannah there. Could be they didn't even know her mother lived there, too."

"So why didn't they just kill her mother?" Ayden asked. "Or abduct or subdue her while they waited for Hannah to come home?"

"Maybe since she'd called the police, getting the advantage, they changed tactics. They trashed the house to add insult to injury as a warning to let Hannah know they can get to her loved ones."

Ayden furrowed his brow. "That would make more sense if there was some kind of demand for information."

"Maybe they have made their demands, and Hannah knows, but we don't. And if that's the case, then what do you think they want?"

"Hannah was trying to find that out tonight when she went to Stevens's office," he told Brett. "But she left the memory drive there."

"What if she went there *because* of those demands? Maybe they asked her to retrieve information for them."

"If that was the case, why did they even come to the bank building?"

Brett shrugged. "There's something else at

play here that we're missing, and we don't know much as it is. But if she left the drive there, then that could mean the attackers have it now. So maybe their attacks will stop."

Ayden wished it was so, for Hannah and her mother's sake, but at the same time, they also needed answers. They needed for the assailants to make a mistake. Who was the man who led the attack on the Greenco offices anyway? Ayden had gotten a glimpse of his face. Before he could think more about the man leading the charge tonight, Hannah stepped out of the hospital room. Frowning, she rubbed her arms. She had been through so much already. She'd just gotten released herself only to turn around and come right back for her mother.

God, when will this end?

Lifting her gaze to him, she edged closer but stopped short of leaning into him. He might have pulled her into his arms, but Brett was there watching the two of them. Gauging Ayden's reaction. Ayden knew he was on the verge of crossing a line here. He was protecting her. Getting involved could cloud a person's judgment. Probably too late for that. He steeled himself against the need to comfort her. The want…

She hurt you, man. She'll do it again.

But was this the time to hold back compassion and comfort?

"How is she?" Brett asked Hannah.

Ayden was too tongue-tied. Idiot.

"She's fine. She was just scared when someone broke into the house. They keep saying her vitals are good, but they were saying that before we brought her here."

"You made the right decision insisting that a doctor check her out," Ayden told her. "Anyone could see she was struggling."

"Thanks for saying that," she murmured, turning toward him. "One thing is for sure, she's ready to get out of here. I'm glad we brought her here as a precaution, but she's okay…well, as okay as someone with a terminal diagnosis can be. She's smiling and reading her Bible, which always comforts her. When the doctor comes by in a bit, we'll ask for her to be released. But…" She lifted her gaze to Ayden again and locked onto his eyes as if she was looking for a measure of hope there.

He searched for hope himself.

"You want to know where we're taking you after she's released," Brett said.

Once again, Ayden hadn't been able to find the words. Hannah continued to hold Ayden's gaze, but nodded in answer to Brett's statement.

"Thank you for agreeing to go somewhere safe," Ayden finally managed.

Her green eyes shimmered with emotion. "I

don't have a choice. I couldn't live with myself if something happened to my mother because of me. Because I brought danger to her."

She pressed her back against the wall and shuddered. "I didn't ask for any of this. All I wanted was to do a good job. Make her proud. Get a promotion and make more money so we could go on our cruise." She chuckled and rubbed her eyes then studied the floor, though her mind had to be miles away. "Can you believe it? She wants to take that cruise through the Inside Passage to Juneau. We've been dreaming. Planning. We need to do this before she's too sick to go. She'll be done with infusions soon. I made the reservations, but of course, we can't know how her health will be. And now, there's so much more going on that I've lost hope we'll even be able to go."

When she looked up at him, her smile was brilliant, and held so much love for her mother. She was beautiful, and truly...the best person he knew. He didn't know why she'd broken things off with him, but he would stop blaming her for that, or harboring anger. She'd committed no crime, and maybe he just wasn't the man for her.

But she didn't seem to have a significant other—and if she did, where was he?

He couldn't help himself and took her hand. "It's going to be okay, Hannah. We've made arrangements for you and your mother to stay in separate places, at least to start."

Her eyes widened, then she slowly nodded. "I understand. I want to do whatever it takes to keep her safe, but she's not going to like it."

ELEVEN

Hannah hated the moment she'd had to say goodbye to her mother. Brett and Caine had wheeled Momma out of the hospital in a wheelchair, and Hannah had stayed behind.

But just before they had wheeled her through the doors, she squeezed Hannah's hand and said, "Remember, sweetheart, the name of the Lord is a strong tower."

"I'll remember, Momma."

No matter what came her way, Momma's faith in God remained strong. And that bolstered Hannah, too. The rest of the scripture came to mind that said the righteous run into the tower and are safe. Had God sent Ayden and his siblings to keep them safe? It would seem so.

Her mother was now well on her way to the prepared safe house and Ayden waited with Hannah for their transportation in the shadows in the hospital parking garage.

Exiting the hospital was safer for Momma if

she went alone, separate from Hannah, whose presence might draw attention to her mother. Whoever had entered the house had probably thought it was empty, and if Hannah had been the target, she didn't think they realized her mother was living at the house. But she couldn't be sure about anything that was going on. She was just grateful her mother was alive. Momma said that the two intruders wore masks…so maybe they did know that someone was at home and hadn't wanted to be identified.

Her heart thrashed around at the thought of Momma in danger. So as much as she hadn't wanted to go to a safe house, she was beyond relieved that her mother would be protected, she'd be safe—at least from dangerous men.

Though Hannah couldn't be sure about who had broken into the house, if it was the same men who were at the bank building tonight—could they have been searching for something, believing the Hannah kept the item at the house? She'd bring that up to Ayden later.

Wheels squealed, echoing through the parking garage, letting them know their ride was on the way. An older-model SUV with dark windows slowed to a stop.

"That's for us." Ayden pressed his hand at the small of her back and ushered her forward. He opened the door, and she climbed into the back seat and buckled in.

This was a bigger vehicle. Big enough to protect her while hiding her.

It's going to be okay. She had to believe that.

Ayden got in the back with her this time, while Everly drove. He seemed to know she wanted him next to her. Wanted him close. Protection emanated from him.

She peered out the window trusting that her mother would be okay and prayed this nightmare would end soon.

Sitting next to Ayden, she realized that the fear, the terror seemed to decrease, if only a little. But unfortunately, each moment she spent with him the truth about what happened before fought to come out.

She chewed on her bottom lip. Telling him the truth about nine years ago was the least of either of their concerns. Really. But she hated keeping secrets. Hated that he must think the absolute worst of her—that she led him on and then broke it off with him. Or maybe he wasn't thinking about that at all. Perhaps what she saw in his eyes that led her to believe he still remembered the pain she'd caused was only in her imagination.

But regardless, coming clean and telling him the truth would devastate him.

"Where are we going?" she asked.

"A hotel for now. Even the US Marshals primarily use hotels as safe houses while protecting witnesses."

"A hotel, huh." If she had to spend hours with Ayden stuck in a small room, she just might go crazy.

"Ayden, there's something we need to talk about." Then again, getting it all off her chest now would remove the burden, the pressure she felt. The pain and reminders, every time she looked at him.

If he knew…

Why was she thinking about that now? Her life was in danger. Her *mother's* life was in danger, too. In fact, anyone near her could be in peril. And she didn't even know why!

Ayden grabbed her hand and squeezed. "Breathe, Hannah."

She closed her eyes and rested her head against the seat back. He was right.

"What's bothering you? What did you want to talk about?"

She blew out a long breath. *Get it over with.* "We never talked about cost. How much am I going to owe you for protecting me when this is over?"

Well, those weren't the words she'd meant to say at all, but too late to take them back now.

He squeezed her hand again, drawing her attention. She took in his warm brown eyes that could turn dark and intense or, like now, soothe her soul with his concern and compassion.

A furrow grew between his brows. "Nothing. You don't owe us anything."

"But this is your business."

"You didn't ask for help. You didn't sign any documents. I… I'm not here because of my company. I thought you knew that. Thought we had already settled that. I'm here because there's no way I'll let you go through this alone."

His words held so much meaning in them, or was she reading him wrong? That he still cared *deeply* for her. She didn't think she was.

Her throat constricted. She could barely get out the words. "Thank you."

Lord, protect Momma, and all those who are bent on protecting us.

But please also protect my heart.

Palpable relief swept over Ayden when he and Everly finally settled Hannah in the hotel room. It was more of a suite, including a nice spacious bedroom, a kitchenette and a connecting room, which he would remain in to protect her. Meanwhile his team would continue to work on threat analysis in case of possible additional attacks, while remaining in close contact with investigators.

And he was grateful to have a serious situation to distract him from the more personal thoughts about Hannah that seemed to be a constant bombardment. A moment later, a knock came at his door, and he readied his weapon.

"It's me," Everly said.

He swung the door open and she waltzed in, holding paper sacks, Caine on her heels. "As promised, I brought groceries, and some personal items for Hannah."

She knocked lightly on the half-open door to Hannah's room. "It's Everly, bearing gifts."

Hannah slid the door completely open; her tired eyes suddenly grew bright when she spotted the bags. "Oh, thank you, Everly. I'm starving!"

Caine followed and set more sacks on the table in her room. "We bought groceries so you can whip up something in the kitchenette, but we also bought Subway sandwiches to eat right away. I'm sure everyone is famished."

Everly turned her attention on Ayden. "Let's eat up quickly, then you and I need to talk."

He cracked half a smile at his take-charge sister, commanding him as if he weren't running the company. But he appreciated her input. "Challenge accepted."

She arched a brow and chuckled. "I wouldn't

think eating quickly would be a challenge for you."

"I was referring to our talk afterward."

"What? You're not scared of me." She chuckled again.

He was glad she kept a good attitude, because maybe he was a little afraid of her. He had a feeling she was going to complicate an already awkward situation. They finished their sandwiches then Hannah and Everly emptied the sacks and stocked the kitchenette.

"Thanks so much, everyone, for getting all this. And thank you, Everly, for the clothes. While I appreciate all your efforts to keep me safe, I can honestly say I hope I won't be here long enough to eat all these groceries or wear all the clothes you bought."

His sister smiled. "Hey, there's only three outfits in the bag. Two pairs of jeans and a pair of sweats. Some shirts. But I agree with you. We hope this won't take too long, but we might as well be prepared."

Hannah sagged at Everly's last words. "I'll pay you back."

She turned her back on them and Ayden hadn't missed the welling tears, but he would give her space. Hannah cleaned off the counter then started heating water to make tea.

While Caine finished off a second bag of

chips to go with his foot-long sub, Everly caught Ayden's hand and pulled him into the other room, leaving the door half-open again. Privacy, but not too much. Hannah might not feel comfortable alone with Caine, though at some point, protecting someone could mean being alone in a room with them.

His sister moved to the window and peered out the curtains at the landscape. They'd chosen a hotel out of town, but they could still see Mt. Rainier in the distance. So many days the mountain couldn't be seen for the low-lying clouds.

"So," she began, "Caine is going to stay with her."

The words stunned him. He took a breath, then, "What?"

"Keep your voice down." With the way she said the words, he was surprised she hadn't added *you big oaf.*

"*I'm* watching Hannah. Protecting her. *Me.* There's no discussion here."

"I'm afraid I have to put my foot down on this."

"I said it's not up for discussion."

"Really? Is that what you meant when you invited us to join you at Honor Protection Specialists? To work as a team?"

"What does this situation have to do with working as a team? Hannah…she's—"

"Exactly. You proved my point. You're too close to this, to her, and you know it. Brett and Caine have seen how you are around her too and they agree you're not on top of your game when she's near."

He scraped a hand through his hair, not liking the fact that his siblings weren't willing to ignore what he kept pushing aside. Still... "I'm the best person to protect her."

"Because you still have a thing for her?"

"*What?* No."

"The fact that you still have a thing for her is the very reason you are not the best person to protect her."

"There are pros and there are cons. I'll agree." Even if he found her attractive, and her emerald green eyes could pull him down and under and keep him there, he knew deep down... "No one will truly protect her the way I would in the direst of circumstances."

Disappointment swept over Everly's features. "That's not fair, Ayden. Untrue and unfair. We're trained to protect with our lives."

"Caine and Brett?"

"I've already said they agree with me." She took a step closer. "Look, last night you were more than willing to let someone else sit in a vehicle and watch the house."

Had that only been last night? So much had happened it seemed like much longer.

"That was yesterday. This is today. Everything has changed."

"Caine is staying the rest of today with her, and I'll stay tonight. Do this for us and we'll talk again tomorrow. I don't think you can make a good judgment call, a good decision without some space and rest. We're your partners, your siblings. Trust us."

He had the feeling that if he didn't give in to her request, he would only be asking for more trouble.

He could trust his siblings with Hannah but... "Only for twenty-four hours."

TWELVE

The next morning, Hannah got dressed then grabbed a large mug of hot steaming coffee. Poured in all the fixings—compliments of Everly. She thought after the two days she'd had she would sleep for a week, but she hadn't slept much at all, and was exhausted. The coffee would help bring her back to life.

She moved toward the window, hoping to look at the mountain, but then she remembered she'd been instructed not to look out the window—for her own protection, of course. And she knew the safety measures were for those who guarded her as well. She'd been allowed to talk to Momma last night via the burner phone Everly left with her.

And she called her mother again this morning.

"Hannah, you're up so early. Are you okay?" Momma sounded surprisingly rested.

"I'm okay as long as you are. You sound good. Did you sleep well?"

"Yes. I had a nice conversation with Ayden. He's such a nice young man. I'm surprised you never mentioned you were friends to me before."

Hannah cringed. What had he told her? "Have they figured out your infusions schedule yet?"

"Oh, yes, no problem. One of them will transport me to a different facility, already authorized. Please, Hannah, you have to stop worrying about me. Just trust in God. He has put these wonderful people in your life to protect you."

"Okay, Momma. I'll try." A soft knock came at the door that separated the two rooms. "I have to go. I'll talk to you later."

"Okay. Be safe and take care of yourself."

"I'm sorry about everything," Hannah couldn't help but add.

"Pffft. God will find a way to work all of this for our good. You wait and see."

Hannah ended the call, wishing for the thousandth time she had her mother's strong faith. She slid the door open to find Everly. Caine had stayed at the hotel with her for the remainder of the day yesterday, and Everly had stayed through the night.

"Did you sleep?" Hannah asked.

"I sleep with one eye open when I'm protecting someone."

"Really? Well, you look wide-eyed and alert."

The woman was beautiful. "So…who's coming today?" *Please say Ayden.*

"Either Caine or Brett."

Hannah frowned and turned then walked to the kitchen. "You want some coffee or eggs or croissants?" She waved her hand with a flourish. "It's your food, after all."

Everly followed her into her room. "You seem disappointed that Ayden isn't coming."

She was that obvious? And how did she answer the woman when she didn't know why she should be disappointed?

A hand pressed her shoulder. "I'm sorry, Hannah." Everly tugged eggs out of the mini-fridge. "I'll scramble eggs. There's bacon too. I don't usually eat like this, but I'm in the mood for something hearty to go with my appetite."

"I should cook for *you*. After all, you guys are protecting me, watching out for me. And I'm not exactly sure why. It's not like I can pay you."

"First, I'll cook. I'm sorry to say you don't look like you slept that well, and I don't want my breakfast ruined." Everly sent her a chuckle and winked. "Second, you know why we're doing this. We care about you. *Ayden* cares about you. Even if he didn't, I can't see him not filling in the gap, working pro bono for someone in need."

Everly put bacon on a plate and into the microwave, and then she cracked the eggs against a frying pan and scrambled them. She angled toward Hannah. "He's not here because I asked him not to be. He cares for you too much, Hannah, and I don't want to see him get hurt again. It really crushed my brother after you broke things off with him. He left and we didn't see him again until six months ago."

Hearing the news from Everly felt like a fist to her heart. She couldn't breathe, much less speak. Or even defend herself for her actions.

Everly plated the eggs and bacon and set it before Hannah along with a plate for herself. She sat at the table across from Hannah. "But that's all I'm going to say. I'm just being a little protective of my brother, I guess, in this situation. But I'm a professional and personal feelings have no place here."

Ayden's sister cleared her throat, bowed her head, and Hannah joined her as she said grace.

"Now, you might have lost your appetite, but this could be a long day. Trust me when I say you should eat while you can."

A knock came at the door to the other room. Everly brandished her gun and gave Hannah a warning look, which she took to mean to stay there but remain alert.

Hannah heard a familiar voice speak with Everly and relief whooshed through her.

Ayden stepped into her room and smiled. Did

he have any idea how glad she was to see him? She had no right to be glad, and she'd certainly received a warning from Everly, whom she didn't blame. Ayden's sister cared about him.

And unfortunately, Hannah realized *she* also cared about him. Still.

Everly's eyes held a challenge. Ayden knew she didn't like that he'd been the one to show up at the hotel to relieve her. Had she really expected him to wait a full twenty-four hours before coming back to task? Oh, that's right, she thought they would *discuss* it after twenty-four hours. But Ayden had no plans for a big confab over whether he should protect Hannah.

He'd gotten rest, sort of, and there was no way he could stay away. But both women stared at him as if waiting for an explanation. He was good with that.

He stole a slice of bacon from his sister's plate and chewed. "There's a change in plans, ladies."

Fists on her hips, Everly arched a brow. "Where's Caine?"

"He's securing the getaway vehicle."

His sister dropped her hands. "What's going on? Why didn't you tell me?"

"This morning I rode with him, so the three of us could talk—" he glanced at Hannah "—I mean all of us. But as we approached the hotel, we spied a suspicious vehicle circling. I think we've been made. Don't ask me how."

Hannah's eyes grew wide. "What about my mother? Is she okay?"

"Brett is preparing to take her to get her infusions. From there, we're arranging for a new hotel."

"We can't live like this." Hannah pushed her plate away and stood to pace. At least this room was big enough for that. "What is it they want from me?"

"We'll figure it out, but in the meantime, we have to go," Everly said. "We'll leave everything. I can get it later. But right now, you're coming with me."

Ayden shook his head. "Change of plans. Caine and I have talked. I'm taking Hannah to Base Camp."

"The old family log cabin at the base of Mt. Rainier?" Everly glanced at Hannah. "It's not a camp like the name implies, so don't worry, but a log cabin in the woods was as close to camping as mom would ever get."

"It's secluded. Nobody will find her there since the cabin was donated to a charity organization, but we're free to use it as needed. It makes a perfect safe house." Ayden and his siblings had met at the cabin for a weekend and that was where they'd discussed and planned out Honor Protection Specialists.

Everly's mouth opened, but no words came out, then she finally said, "Fine. You two get out of here. I'll follow with the groceries and the extra clothes. Don't worry. No one will follow me."

"Be careful." Ayden gave his sister a hug. She returned the hug and when she released him, her expression appeared entirely too emotional—for her.

He texted Caine, who called him back.

"Give me ten minutes. I'll text when I get there, but my plan is to wait at the back exit. If you come down now, we should be all clear. I've secured a white Mavis Electric and Plumbing utility van."

Ayden almost laughed. His brother had a special gift for securing resources. "Everly will wait in the room for you to come get her and help carry out her purchases."

He ended the call and filled the women in on his phone call with Caine. Everly nodded as she wiped down the counter because she didn't want to leave the hotel room a mess. Typical Everly. "Do we know anything more about who's behind this? Are the police any closer to catching the men?" Hannah asked.

Ayden had spent the night at his office but

hadn't been able to sleep for thinking about the men after her. He'd spoken with Detective Lincoln Mann again, too. "We're making headway."

She shot him a look. "Really? How so?"

"Well, for starters, Stevens's office is now a crime scene. The man leading the other two storming into the building wasn't wearing a mask, so his face was caught on security cameras—before they were destroyed. Maybe he hadn't planned for that, so we have that. Lincoln will send the image to me once he gets clearance." He blew out a breath. "I saw the guy too, but only briefly. Camera footage will be a bigger help. Facial recognition software can help to identify him."

"And what about the USB?" Everly interjected. "Have you tracked it down?"

"It wasn't there," he replied. "We have to assume they took it. The computer has been taken by forensic techs."

"It's possible they could find out what the men are after in addition to identifying the leader," Hannah said.

He scraped his jaw. "Maybe."

She stepped closer. "What is it? What are you thinking?"

"If all they wanted was something on Stevens's system, it seems like they could hack into it. Find another way." Brett was right when he'd said something more was at play here.

God, what is it?

"And…you think I know something," Hannah said. "I assure you I don't."

"Well, keeping thinking on it. You were closer to him than anyone regarding his company. If anyone knows anything, it has to be you." And obviously the men targeting her believed that, too.

He studied her, searching her eyes for any deception. But that was stupid. He believed she'd been telling the truth.

The thing was, he still got the sense she was hiding something.

THIRTEEN

A seat had been anchored awkwardly in the back of the van, to which she was strapped in. Hannah gripped the seat as Ayden drove the utility van along a state highway.

The van seemed to shake and rattle with every imperfection in the road, jarring her teeth more than once. The ride was uncomfortable, and they'd been on the road for longer than she would think necessary.

"Anyone following us?"

"Not so far. I won't head toward the cabin until I'm absolutely sure."

Ayden had explained they would be driving for a while so he could make sure to lose any tails, but Hannah was more than ready to get out of here.

"What? You mean we've been driving for an hour in the wrong direction?" She couldn't help but tease him, though there was a real question in her jest.

"Yep. Haven't you ever taken the long way around?"

"Momma calls that the scenic route. And yes, I've taken the scenic route. I've also gotten lost a few times."

"Lost. I didn't think people did that anymore in this age of Google Maps and GPS."

"Ha ha. You're funny. Do you think it would be okay if I moved up front with you?"

"Here." He tossed a Mariners ball cap back to her. She tucked her hair under it to continue the covert mission to safety, then unbuckled, and slipped from the uncomfortable seat in the back. Hannah held on to the seat, gripped the back of Ayden's. Crawling into the passenger seat wasn't easy, but she made it.

Settling in beside him, she sighed in relief and buckled again. "Thanks for letting me sit up here. I didn't think I could take much more back there."

"That bad, huh?"

"Oh yeah. I don't know why they bothered adding that seat."

Ayden didn't respond, seeming to prefer the quiet. The day had turned rainy, and the forest was thick and dark as it hugged the road. Depressing to some, but she enjoyed this part of living in the Pacific Northwest. Residing in this region of the country meant learning to deal with dreary gray days. And actually, she more than enjoyed it. She *loved* it. Feeling a semblance of peace wash over her, she rested her head against the seat back.

"Did you ever imagine..." She shook her head, unwilling to finish the thought. Wishing she hadn't started it.

"Nope. I never imagined."

Okay, well, she didn't need to finish the thought. He could read her mind. That scared her a little bit. She'd wanted to tell him the truth before but held back because, really, she hadn't been brave enough. And now, in the middle of heading to the family cabin, bringing up his criminal judge father seemed like the absolute wrong thing.

"Have you been thinking about what they could be after?" he asked.

"Look, me being Mr. Stevens's assistant, working closely with him, doesn't mean what you might think. I worked closely with him regarding his schedule, signatures and emails and appointments. So yes, I was really just a glorified administrative assistant. I didn't know much about the actual inner workings, the gears and the internal stuff of the software that he developed. I have a basic understanding at best."

"That's why you were going after the USB, so you could find more," he mused. "I had wondered why you simply didn't log in from your laptop from home."

"I had access to almost everything. I figured there must be files I didn't know about—something worth killing him over."

"Well, let's think outside the box then. About what the Greenco does. Maybe a competitor—"

She shook her head. "No. That seems improbable."

"Maybe. But in my line of work before with the DSS, I saw a lot of corporate crimes that would blow you away."

Hannah rubbed her arms and watched the road, fighting the exhaustion with eyelids that grew heavy. "I just don't want to be in the middle of all this."

"I know."

Or be in the middle of it with Ayden of all people. She turned to look out the passenger window.

Her gaze snagged on the side-view mirror. "Um… Ayden?"

"I see it." Tension edged his tone.

"Are we being followed?" *Please, no.*

"Possibly." He sounded positive with that one word.

Hanna wanted to scream. "How?"

"That's why I took the long way. Eventually, the lurkers will have to come out of the shadows."

"That makes sense, but if the vehicle is following us, what do you do to get rid of them?" A chill crawled over her, then into her bones. Cold and painful.

"That's a fair question."

She swiveled back toward him. "And I'd like an answer."

"I hope I can lose them."

Oh, was that all.

To think, Ayden had almost driven onto the back road that headed toward the mountain and the Base Camp cabin. Fortunately, he'd seen the tail before making the mistake of taking that turn, so he deliberately passed the road. Someone was going to a lot of trouble to get to Hannah.

He had held on to the smallest flicker of hope that the assailants found what they needed in that USB drive and would stop pursuing Hannah, but that hope had been fleeting, at best.

He called Brett. "We've been followed."

"We're still at the hospital," his brother said. "Susan's infusions are almost done. What are you thinking? That someone led you to believe they were onto you, circling the hotel, but someone else had been sitting in the parking lot, watching and waiting for you to make a move?"

"Yep. The old bait and switch version of shadowing someone."

"101."

"I suggest bringing Caine in," Ayden said to Brett, while he glanced at Hannah. "Let's keep her mother moving and switch things up with her."

The last thing he wanted to happen was for the ailing woman to be abducted, held for ransom or…killed. His palms began to sweat against the steering wheel at the thought.

"In the meantime, what are you going to do? How are you going to shake them?"

"I have an idea." A risky one.

"I'll bring Everly into this, too. We'll follow the followers."

"Be careful." He ended the call.

Hannah shrank down in her seat, tugging the ball cap even lower. "So the ball cap thing didn't work."

"I'm afraid they must have been watching the moment we left the hotel. But keep it on, just in case we can lose them."

"What's your plan?" she asked warily.

"I need to get gas, during which time you go into the ladies' room and lock the door. Stay there."

"In a gas station restroom? Ew. No."

He couldn't help but laugh. "Okay. Then I have a better idea."

He contacted Lincoln. "We're being followed. We're in Pierce County now, but could you—"

"I'm on it. We'll get deputies out there to pull him over. Just keep driving."

"I'll need to stop and get gas within the next twenty minutes so please make it fast."

"Will do. Let me know if anything changes."

He hung up. Glanced at Hannah and saw the smile. The admiration in her eyes. What a dummy he was to only now think of calling in for help. Everly was right, being with Hannah definitely affected his abilities. Then he glanced at the side-view mirror.

The grille of that truck grew bigger as the vehicle came closer. "Uh-oh." They were closing in fast. "I have the feeling they're listening to a police scanner."

"What?" She sounded breathless, desperate. "Well, then I would think if they knew deputies were headed this way to pull them over, they would disappear instead of moving in. What are we going to do now? We can't let them catch us."

Ayden's gun was in his holster, and he'd brought extra ammo and guns, but the last thing he wanted was to get into a shootout with these guys while protecting Hannah. Still, he imagined wrapping his hands around the leader's neck and squeezing.

"I'll try to hold them off until law enforcement can catch up and pull them over."

"But Ayden, we'll be endangering their lives."

"I'm glad you care so much, Hannah. But cops are trained to serve and protect. A lot of them live for the moments when they can see the action." He said the words for her benefit, but still prayed no one would be hurt or killed.

Tightly gripping the steering wheel, he focused on the task ahead and increased speed. Hannah was quiet, probably concentrating on the road as if she could will them to safety. He got that.

The vehicle behind them rumbled forward and rammed into his bumper. His head thrust forward and then back. In his peripheral vision, he saw Hannah's do the same. Not enough for whiplash, but anger fueled him. The impact caused the back tires to skid on the wet pavement, and he righted the van. He wasn't driving the faster vehicle, which was working against them. Nor could he outmaneuver the driver pursuing them on a lonely strip of wet highway.

His adrenaline spiked as the truck pulled up next to them on the left, then swerved to bump against them. They jolted to the left and the tires slipped, but he continued forward and kept them on the road. He swerved left to return the favor and hoped their pursuers would head off the road and into the ditch.

A car heading toward them in the opposite lane honked, and their stalker backed down, slowing enough to move back into the right lane. Ayden clenched his jaw and squeezed the steering wheel.

"Hannah, please redial the last number I called on my cell."

She lifted the cell and called. It went to voice mail.

"What should I say?"

"Tell him we're under attack and to hurry."

When the voice mail came on it indicated the voice mailbox was full and could receive no more messages.

He pounded the steering wheel. "Leave a text then."

The other vehicle rammed them again. The cell flew out of Hannah's hands and hit the floorboard.

"Oh, no!" She started to unbuckle in order to reach the cell.

"Leave it!" he shouted. "I'm sorry…just leave it," he said, softer now. "He already knows we're in trouble. He'll see that I called."

Once again, the truck behind them swerved over into the left lane and increased speed until it was next to the van. He veered toward the left to cut the other driver off, fearing he would try to reach the cab and shoot at them. The driver steered the truck into the van hard and fast, barreling into them with enough force this time that Ayden lost control and his vehicle slid off the road and down an embankment.

Hannah screamed.

Ayden prayed and tried to steer the van as it raced toward a tree, but it slammed into the trunk.

FOURTEEN

Hannah gasped for breath and shoved the airbag away.

Her body dazed, she blinked until her mind could wrap around what had just transpired. Steam boiled up out of the front end of the van that was crushed against the tree trunk. Branches hung down around them, as if embracing and shielding them after the crash.

That's right. The bad guys had pursued them. Rammed them down the embankment and into a tree. They could be out there, rushing forward to shoot and kill Hannah and Ayden at any moment. Fear pushed bile up her throat.

Ayden.

Was he all right?

She glanced to her left. His head lulled forward. "Ayden… Ayden! Are you okay?" She unbuckled and shifted closer to shake him.

When he turned toward her, she could see a bloody gash on his forehead, but the fog in his brown eyes seemed to clear and he sucked in a breath.

"Get down, Hannah. Get down."

He grabbed his gun and fired through her window. Glass shattered. Her ears rang with the loud blasts. She covered her head, plugged her ears and listened to the screams.

Coming from her? She could barely hear them.

"Can you get out?" he asked, urgency in his tone, though the words sounded muffled.

"I don't know." She glanced up at him. "Is it safe?"

"For the moment. Why don't you climb over on my side. Please, hurry." He opened his door and backed out, then turned his back to her as he held his gun, ready to protect her.

She crawled over onto the driver's seat, and he offered his free hand. She hopped out.

Sirens rang out and closed in. Relief swept over her, but they weren't out of this yet.

"Let's go." He grabbed her hand and tugged her to the twisted metal at the front of the van and around the tree. "Slide down and get as low as you can."

Ayden peered around the tree. Gunfire rang out again, splintering the tree trunk. Ayden returned fire. Shouts resounded with more gunfire, only this time, it must have been the police or deputies engaging with their stalkers. More gunfire and then an engine roared to life. Tires squealed. Car doors shut and she heard the sound of a vehicle taking off, and another vehicle—with sirens—giving chase.

They were getting away? "Did they leave us?" She started to stand.

"Wait." Ayden gripped her shoulder. "Stay there until I'm sure you're safe."

He peered around the tree and addressed the police officers. "I'm Ayden Honor. I called for assistance."

He stepped out from behind the tree. "Thank you for getting here in time. They ran us off the road and were trying to kill us."

He offered Hannah his hand and she took it, then stepped up behind him. Another siren sounded, growing louder.

A county deputy looked over the crushed front of the van, then at Hannah. His gaze stopped and lingered on Ayden's forehead.

"An ambulance is on the way. Looks like you two need medical assistance."

"Not as much as a new ride," Ayden muttered.

The deputy cocked his head. "Where are you headed?"

"Somewhere safe. Can we give you our statement now? We have to make our way to safety. You can speak to Detective Mann if you need more information."

The deputy nodded and took their statements. They both left out the longer details of their ongoing attacks, but at least there was a record of this incident, and license plate numbers. She would let Ayden worry about any other details the deputy might need.

When they finished the ambulance finally arrived and maneuvered near the edge of the road. Hannah thought she'd sat on a gurney one too many times in her life and hoped she would never have to see a stretcher or an ambulance again. But she was okay. Possible bruising across her chest, but she did not want to go back to the hospital for that, after all she'd been through. Going back to the hospital would mean starting this journey over again. A medic put a big white bandage across the gash in Ayden's forehead that, with the blood, looked worse than it was.

He was fortunate the cut wasn't deep enough to require stitches, and he didn't appear to have a concussion.

Eventually Detective Mann showed up, as well. They'd been in one spot long enough. She moved away from the ambulance and leaned against one of the law enforcement vehicles and watched Ayden talking to the detective and one of the deputies.

He seemed to be in his element with them.

She only needed three words to describe Ayden. Strong. Handsome. Protective.

Lord, what am I doing in this mess with him? Are You trying to tell me something?

Momma always quoted that scripture about how all things work together for good to them that love God, to them who were the called according to His purpose. She just couldn't fathom how any of this could turn out good, nor was she sure about His purpose for her, if she even had one.

Ayden stepped away from the detective and deputy, and his gaze found hers, shutting down her thoughts about purposes and things working out. That look he gave her—she couldn't define it…she could only *feel* it, and her throat grew thick and tight. She wasn't sure whether or not her reaction to this man was good or bad.

After the deputy had dropped Ayden off at the nearest small airport, he secured a rental car from a guy who'd known his father, the Judge, and continued on his way to Base Camp. Exhaustion weighed on him—but he had special training, and he could stay awake for days at a time.

Alert and awake.

"How much farther?" Hannah stirred next to

him. She'd fallen asleep and he'd let her—today had been exhausting and trying.

But at least, this time, they hadn't been followed.

"We're almost there." He turned down the long dirt drive—really more of a trail than an actual road. He'd always been surprised the Judge hadn't wanted to pave the drive, but this was more in keeping with nature.

"It's hard to see in the dark, but this is a private drive that will take us to the family cabin."

Since it was summer, everything was thick and green, especially the underbrush that tried to take over the dirt road. Tree branches scraped against the rental vehicle, scratching and clawing at it as if to prevent him from going deeper into the woods. He hoped he could buff any scratches out and this wasn't going to cost him.

"It's kind of creepy. Are you sure this will be a safe place?"

I'm as sure as I can be about anywhere I could take you. Which even to him didn't sound all that reassuring, so he simply said, "Yes."

"I trust you," Hannah murmured. "I mean… things have happened, but you've been there protecting me at every turn. I know that even if they find us out here, you'll be there. I don't want you to get hurt, though, Ayden. I couldn't live with that, if you were harmed because of me."

She sucked in a breath.

An undefinable emotion stabbed through his heart. She'd hurt him before…and it would seem that she had, in fact, lived with it. But she had not been referring to nine years ago with her statement. Still, that painful moment came to mind. If only he could just forget it. But forgetting it would mean forgetting what she'd meant to him.

And maybe that was the crux of it. He couldn't let go, couldn't move on…he couldn't forget what she'd meant to him.

He was a complete and utter fool.

"Ayden, I'm sorry. I didn't mean—"

"It's okay. It's in the past, Hannah." Then why wouldn't what happened before just stay there? He'd survived. *They'd* survived. And he'd moved on—except not romantically. He hadn't been able to trust anyone or risk the hurt that could come with opening up his heart again.

That was on him.

He never thought he would appreciate the cabin as much as he did at this moment, when he pulled into the clearing and there it stood—looking far more like a lodge than a family cabin. But it distracted him from his thoughts. Funny he was trying to push away past heartache, and ignore current attractions and emotional connections, all while taking the very girl at the root of it all to a lone cabin in the woods.

He slowed at the edge of the woods. "There it is. Base Camp."

"*That's* what you call Base Camp?"

He chuckled through the exhaustion. "As Everly mentioned, it's as close to camping as Mom would ever get, and it's at the base of Mt. Rainier, so we kids gave it that name and it kind of stuck over the years."

"What are you doing? Why are we just sitting here at the edge of the woods instead of driving up to the cabin?" Her teeth chattered slightly as if she was cold.

"Just waiting." Watching.

The clouds had cleared out and the silvery moon shined down on the clearing, casting shadows and giving the cabin an ethereal look.

"I don't like this, Ayden. Does someone live here? You said it was the family cabin, but it looks abandoned."

"No one lives here. I was here with Brett a month and a half ago, checking things out."

She propped her hands on her hips. "You don't think the people after me could somehow track us here?"

Anything was possible in this day and age. "Of all the places we could stay, this would be the hardest place to know about. The most difficult to find."

He grabbed her hand and squeezed, hoping

to reassure her, and with the touch he felt her silky soft skin. He eased the vehicle forward to the front door of the house and smiled. He was going to enjoy seeing the surprise on her face. He pulled out his cell.

"You get a signal out here?" she asked.

"You sound surprised."

"We're in the middle of nowhere." She shrugged.

"There's a small town three miles away. And a cell tower nearby." He didn't add that the Judge's influence held a lot of sway even when it came to cell phone tower placement. With his phone, he pulled up an app, then hit the right selections.

The lights in the cabin suddenly came on.

Hannah laughed. "A smart house. Of course!"

He'd let her think he was smart too, but if he were really smart, he would have programmed the house to turn the lights and heat on before they arrived. Still, he didn't want to draw unwanted attention and so it had been best to wait, at least on the lights.

"Let's get inside and settled in. We need to make sure all the mini-blinds are shut and curtains are drawn and keep a very low profile."

"What about the groceries? Our food. Everly was supposed to bring that along with the clothes she bought. Will that risk someone following us here?"

"I called her while at the rental car place.

She's not coming just yet. The cabin is relatively stocked. Canned foods, including chicken and tuna. Pasta. Frozen foods."

Before he caught himself, he shoved a loose lock of hair behind her ear. Too intimate on his part, but she didn't flinch away.

And he wished that she had.

FIFTEEN

Hannah was surprised at how relaxed she felt in the spacious cabin with a warm polished cedar and pine interior and the most comfortable and cozy furniture she'd ever seen. Decorative hand-made quilts on the beds in, what—six bedrooms? This place would make a nice bed-and-breakfast. She and Momma had dreamed about starting one before Momma got sick.

Hannah was beginning to get accustomed to her hopes and dreams being dashed. Almost to the point of trying hard not to have any expectations at all. No expectations meant no disappointments.

And that expectant awareness coursed through her now as she made dinner for Ayden.

Wow. She was cooking dinner for the two of them, and it was surreal. Still, it wasn't a romantic get-together. While he'd brought in his guns and ammo, she'd explored and then found the cabin stocked, just like he'd said. He'd done so much for her, she might as well do a small part, so she'd created a simple pasta dish—spaghetti and marinara sauce. She found some frozen garlic bread, though she wasn't sure how long it had been in the freezer and hoped it didn't have freezer burn. But the aroma filling the kitchen was wonderful, if she said so herself. Also, roasting in the oven was broccoli—overnight she'd become a veritable chef.

Ayden moved around the house, closing all the window coverings to make sure they had privacy and to hide her whereabouts. With her in the kitchen, and Ayden doing "manly" chores, she smiled to herself. An incredulous smile, really.

They might have been standing in this very cabin, doing this very thing as a married couple if she hadn't buckled under the pressure and had made different choices for herself.

She sighed as she strained the pasta.

"What are you thinking?" Ayden's voice was husky, rich and she liked the sound of it. She could almost imagine him coming up behind her and hugging her, his chin at her shoulder, as he watched her finish dinner preparations.

Okay, now she was letting her imagination run too far and in a direction that it should never go—anymore.

"Nothing. Just thinking." She tossed in the

marinara sauce and the broccoli then sprinkled on Parmesan cheese and then plated it.

When she turned, holding a plate for him, she caught him standing against the wall watching her. Her heart palpated and she almost dropped the plate.

"Here…here you go."

He smiled, and dimples emerged, then he stepped forward to take the dish. "Thank you. You didn't have to, you know."

She prepared her own dish then sat at the table where she'd already placed a glass of water for each of them. "I was hungry, okay? And you were right—the place is stocked."

A noise drew her attention and she glanced toward the living room. The kitchen was an open-concept design, but a partial wall separated the two rooms.

"I started a fire. It gets cold up here at night."

She smiled over at him. "A fire sounds nice." To go with their Italian dinner. Why hadn't she thought to put on music to add to the ambiance?

"I thought so, too," he said, then bowed his head and said grace for them.

Afterward, she swirled spaghetti onto her fork and glimpsed at him. She expected him to have that preoccupied look on his face—thinking through protecting her and their next steps—but he seemed uncomfortable.

"A fire in the fireplace. An Italian dinner. Ayden, is this…" What *is* this? Had this been his plan all along—although she'd been the one to make dinner. No. She was tired. She wasn't thinking right.

When he lifted his gaze, his brown eyes sparked with questions of his own. And she absolutely couldn't finish what she was going to say. He hadn't planned this. Of course, he hadn't. But could this pseudoconversation—or this moment—get any *more* awkward?

He continued to look at her as if waiting for more before he responded.

Smart man. Oh, she got it, all right. He was afraid that whatever he said would be the wrong answer. And oddly, the very idea of that sent warmth spiraling through her.

Ayden's cell rang and he took the call, excusing himself, for which she was grateful. She exhaled in relief.

She'd been hungry and making them both dinner seemed the right thing to do. After all, he was protecting both her and her mother, and all pro bono—as Everly had mentioned. Why? Out of duty? Or because he cared about her?

But she hadn't meant to create a romantic ambiance, which she'd inadvertently done, just as he'd done with the fire. By the time he came back from his call, she'd washed her plate and cleaned the pans. He stared at the remaining food on his dish in dismay.

"Are you done? I wasn't sure, and I had finished so—"

"It's all right." He took a few bites from his plate. She'd warmed it up for him. "It's delicious. Thank you."

Heat rushed to her cheeks, and she turned to add hot water to the sink for his dish.

He scraped the remaining food into the garbage then thrust it into the dishwater and she finished washing. She hadn't expected him to stand so close and stepped away.

"Why not use the dishwasher?" he asked.

"I hope we're not going to be here long enough to run an entire load in the dishwasher."

"Smart thinking. I hope you're right." Another call came through and he excused himself once again.

What was going on? If he didn't tell her once he got back, she'd have to ask. She headed into the living room to stare at the crackling fire. Warm. Cozy.

Though she'd preferred his company to Caine's or Brett's, or even Everly's, that was before she was in a cabin with him with a fire blazing.

Romantic.

She could imagine this place as a honeymoon getaway. Hannah dropped onto a plush, comfy love seat and watched the flames, while she listened to the low tones of his voice in the hallway. She'd love to listen in, but then again, she was almost too tired to care. A slight noise drew her around and she saw Ayden had taken a spot on the sofa across from her.

He half smiled. "Sorry about that. Dinner was amazing, by the way. Thank you."

She laughed. "You tease me."

"I wouldn't lie to you. I loved it. You never cooked for me before." His smile suddenly flattened.

Oh, boy. And there it was, that big fat elephant in the room come to taunt them while they were in this romantic cabin to keep her safe.

He'd set all the alarms. Security cameras were on and he could access those with his phone. Everything was encrypted and free from hackers. The Judge wouldn't have had it any other way.

So he could breathe while he was here alone protecting Hannah.

But what had he been thinking building the fire?

The romantic ambiance—no, make that serious heavy tension—filled the room. When he'd been here before with his family and with his siblings, he never once imagined the place could feel like this.

But he'd never brought Hannah here.

And now…now he would have to remember that he had even considered bringing her here to propose.

Idiot.

She watched him. Could she read his mind? Maybe she didn't have to since he'd put his foot in his mouth with that reference to their past. He should hop right up and pace or check the perimeter. Something.

But her eyes were bright and luminous and the flames…he was pretty sure that if he was closer, he would see gold dancing around inside the green. The thought caused his breath to catch. And before he realized he'd done it, he was in the chair positioned diagonal next to the sofa. He pulled it up closer to her.

Near enough he could touch her hair.

She angled her head slightly and looked at him out of the corners of her eyes. Would his nearness disturb her? In a bad way, that was. Or would she welcome it?

In her eyes he saw the beautiful, vibrant colors that he'd expected, hoped to see. His heart pounded.

A headiness wrapped around him. He was a fool and inched away, sitting back against the chair.

Returning the chair to its original position

now would be ridiculous. Fortunately, she looked back to the fire, removing her captivating gaze from his reach.

God, what do I do now? Why am I here with this woman I once loved? This woman I had wanted to marry? Why are You torturing me?

But was it torture, really?

Yes. Definitely, yes.

But she held something close. A secret. And he would have it now.

"Hannah." He spoke softly and gently so he wouldn't shift the ambiance too much. *Why didn't you ever take me to meet your mother?* "Tell me about your father."

He'd dated her for a year, and thought he knew her. But now, after meeting her mother, he realized he'd been in love with a woman he hadn't known at all. And he wanted to know her. For her own protection, maybe, but deep down, because he wanted to know what went wrong before.

Her shoulders lifted and then drooped with a heavy sigh. "What's to tell, really? He was an alcoholic."

"I'm so sorry. I assume that…he died. He's gone. Or are your parents divorced?" The man hadn't seemed to be around.

"Liver failure. He… It pains me to say this, but I wasn't sad when he died. He would come home drunk and terrorize us. Beat my mother. It was…awful."

Ayden wanted to reach over and—do what, he wasn't sure. They were close enough. He would sit right here. In a few minutes he would check the windows. The cameras. He would protect them from more than physical dangers.

"Mom worked hard as a single mother. She was a waitress at a diner about half a mile away. She would walk to and from work every day except Sunday. Mac, her boss, was good to her and let her off on Sunday so she could go to church. But it was hard, Ayden. You grew up…differently. You had money."

"I—"

"Let me finish. I'm not condemning your lifestyle, or judging you, nothing like that. I'm just saying you can't understand the hardships I've been through." She glanced his way with a smile then, and he saw tears shining in her eyes.

Oddly—they were happy tears.

He smiled back at her, emotion flooding his chest.

"But it was okay. Momma and I had each other. We loved each other. We made it work. She always told me to reach for the stars and tried to plant ridiculously huge dreams in my mind early on."

He tore his gaze away. It was too much to

look at the love and admiration, the dreams—
he could see it all in her eyes.

And those beautiful green eyes had been the
very thing to draw him in from the first moment
he saw her.

Was it happening all over again? It couldn't
happen again. He wouldn't let it.

"She told me I could be anything, do anything." She chuckled—well, a half chuckle,
half choking on tears. "I admit, I should have
dreamed bigger."

She turned to him and laughed. Hard.

He couldn't help but join in. And said, through
his laughter, "I have no idea why we're laughing."

Which made her laugh even harder.

It was a few moments before she managed to
speak again.

"I think I'm just slap-happy, as my mother
likes to say. I don't know why we're laughing,
either."

"Well, you said you hadn't dreamed big
enough and then you totally lost it."

She snickered. Yep. She was definitely exhausted.

"Come on, I could have reached for the stars
like she said. I could have tried to be an astronaut. Instead, I ended up being a glorified secretary."

With someone trying to kill you.

He didn't say the words and wished he hadn't thought of them.

Then again, he had a job to do.

SIXTEEN

I'm just an administrative assistant. Okay, well, she'd been more than that, but still, what did they want with her?

She smiled again. "And if I was an astronaut, nobody would be trying to kill me. Nobody could reach me, even if they wanted to."

Another laugh burst from her. This was all so ridiculous and surreal, she couldn't help herself.

"I'm trying to make it so they can't reach you now, Hannah." His voice was gentle and sounded like the Ayden she'd known before, and unfortunately reminded her of their past. The good times. The man she'd fallen in love with. But their time together was gone, and now they were two proverbial ships passing in the night. They had this moment, but it wouldn't last.

If she even survived.

She stared at the flames, aware that he was mere inches from her. She'd soaked in his laughter, his presence. His goodness.

No. He was nothing like his father.

"It was a dream come true the day I got the job to work under Kristen and train to work closely with such a high-profile, up-and-coming businessman—Alfred Stevens was brilliant."

Ayden shifted in the chair a little. Was it her imagination, or was he jealous that she'd praised the man? What did it matter?

"Kristen trained me but I was not prepared to take over quite so quickly. However, she was pregnant and suddenly prescribed bed rest for the term of her pregnancy so I had no choice in the matter."

"I'm sure you did a great job." Ayden was only trying to reassure her. He couldn't know one way or another.

"Then the pressure was on. Kristen left some big shoes to fill."

He said nothing to that and she listened to the crackling fire and let it mesmerize her. The blaze could lull her to sleep, and she was much too comfortable now. She'd been telling Ayden her sad sob story, and if she wasn't careful, she might tell him more.

Not now. Maybe never.

The room suddenly grew stuffy, and his nearness…stifling. Hannah rose from the love seat and moved to the window. She pulled the shade he'd drawn back enough to see outside. Was someone lurking out there, preparing to break into the cabin to get to her, and if so, why?

Ayden would surely scold her. Pull her away.

In the meantime, she would stare out into the silvery night. The rich greenery around the cabin. The moon had shifted just out of sight. The clouds reflected the light as they creeped across the sky. The top of the mountain was silhouetted against the night sky and this close to it, she could only see a portion.

On a gasp, she drew back.

Stepping right into Ayden's chest.

Another gasp and she almost turned around, but he held her in place. And just like she'd imagined him doing while she was at the stove in the kitchen, he held her against him and peered over her shoulder into the night. Her heart pounded.

She knew her quickened breaths would give away how he affected her. But she was caught up in an ethereal bubble, floating on the sensations as he held her. Though she couldn't let herself fall for him again, at this moment, there was nothing she could do to break away. If all she had with him was this moment, she would take it.

It was like a dream.

She didn't want it to end.

He slowly turned her around.

What are you doing? But those thoughts

wouldn't surface on her lips. He peered at her, one question in his eyes.

And in answer she leaned in, warmth humming through her entire body.

Her throat constricted, her breathing hitched, and anticipation flooded through her. She stared at his lips, aching for him to kiss her. She leaned closer, and then it happened. He pressed gently against her lips, not demanding, but hungry and holding back at the same time. Emotion... powerful emotion surged through her to him, and she was sure he felt it, too. Heat tingled over her skin.

She brushed her hands across his strong chest, up the muscles cording his arms and neck, and then weaved her fingers through his thick hair.

Hannah was in his arms. And *he* was in her arms. Her fingers traced over his face up into his hair, and though he held her, he was the true captive. He wanted to deepen the kiss, but eased back, though he didn't release her. Not yet.

He hadn't realized that there was a big dark abyss, a hole in his heart, that had remained open and hurting this whole time since she'd dumped him. With her in his arms, the pain eased, if only for a brief moment.

This shouldn't happen. It couldn't last.

Pain spilled out of his heart, pouring out and

rushing to his brain, and he would have pulled away, except a groan escaped her throat and he was lost forever in her arms.

A buzz rattled through him, stirring the warnings in his head.

Again and again.

His *cell*...it was buzzing.

Hannah eased back, but it felt like she'd torn her lips from him. "Are you...are you going to get that?" The question came out breathy.

Then she pulled away completely, her arms slowly dropping down to his shoulders and over his chest as she eased away, as if she too regretted having to step back. The abyss, the hole in his chest widened again as she pulled away.

"Your cell, Ayden."

Her eyes held his, but he shook off the moment, or tried to and cleared his throat. He reached for the phone to glance at the number. Everly.

Oh. Man. Everly. Of course, she had to be calling at this moment as if she had some sort of instinct about Ayden and Hannah. And if Everly knew...she would be furious.

He couldn't blame her. He was furious at himself. "It's my sister."

"Are you going to call her back?"

He pulled Hannah from the window. "Yes, but first..." He hung his head. Shame engulfed him.

God, why am I such a fool? But he would own it. "Hannah, it's not my intention—" he cleared his throat "—never my intention to take advantage of someone. Someone who is in a vulnerable position."

"I'm not vulnerable. I… I can make my own—"

"You're exhausted. We're both exhausted. Please, don't take this the wrong way." He squeezed his eyes shut. "With everything in me, I wanted to kiss you. But I shouldn't have let it go that far. It shouldn't have happened. Please forgive me."

"I kissed you back, Ayden. I wanted the kiss, too. Maybe…we both wanted it and it was good to get it out of the way, so we can move on. Oh, wow, that didn't sound right."

He grinned at her words because he totally got it. The problem was one kiss would not let them simply move on. Unfortunately, being here at the safe house with her would be even harder now. "Everly is on the way. She's…just up the road."

"Well, I suppose that's a relief for both of us. She'll keep us in line."

"Yes, she will."

"We both made a mistake, Ayden. No hard feelings. We know that nothing can ever come from this." Her voice hitched when she said those last words.

Did she have those kinds of thoughts about him? Something more? A future? She'd blown that chance nine years ago.

Ayden sighed, because he could see a future with her, except for the fact that he could never trust her again.

God, I don't know what I'm going to do if the bad guys aren't caught in the next few days. Or hours.

But that wasn't true, either. Ayden knew exactly what he would do. He would protect Hannah, and he would assist in the investigation in any way he could, and then he would move on with his life.

With a big gaping hole in his heart that never seemed to heal.

SEVENTEEN

Hannah yawned and stretched and rolled to her side. Sunlight spilled from the small space between the wall and curtains. She stretched again and stared at the ceiling—the knots in the cedar logs. Beautiful.

Had she really slept?

Last night, she'd fallen into bed exhausted, but that heady kiss had stayed with her until she'd fallen asleep. Had Ayden ever kissed her like that before? She couldn't recall, and she would think she would remember a lip-lock like that.

But more ridiculous was that it didn't matter. They'd discussed it like two reasonable adults, knowing that there could be nothing between them.

The words made perfect sense. They were true, so of course they would make sense.

But still, the words had felt wrong, whereas the kiss had felt wonderfully right.

Everly had shown up moments later and had

brought Hannah's clothes, reassuring them a thousand times she hadn't been followed. Hannah showered and dressed. Brushed her teeth and hair, wishing she had some makeup, just a little, then she realized—why? Why would she want to fix herself up?

Ayden.

He was burrowing under her skin and into her heart, but truly she'd never completely rid herself of him. She'd simply pushed thoughts and feelings for him into a vault and locked them away. But that kiss…

A knock came at the door. "It's Everly, Hannah. Are you up yet?"

Hannah swung the door open and smiled. "You cooked breakfast again?"

"Yep. But it's been sitting there for a while. I thought I'd let you sleep in, but I heard you moving around."

"Breakfast sounds good. Coffee even better."

Everly turned and bounded down the steps. Hannah followed, trying once again to shake thoughts of the kiss.

She slowly descended the staircase and saw the display of food on the big kitchen counter. A man stood against the counter. Sixties maybe. Lean with leathery, weathered skin. Sharp eyes. He nodded as he drank from a coffee cup.

"This is Kenny," Everly said.

Wary, Hannah nodded back at him and climbed onto a tall seat where a plate of food waited. Everly poured her coffee. Hannah turned her way and smiled. "You didn't have to cook me breakfast, you know, but I appreciate it."

Everly waved. "Please. No one lets me pamper them. I love to do it when I get the chance."

She studied Hannah long and hard until she felt uncomfortable. Finally, she said, "Kenny is a recently retired detective. He knew both my parents and we've known him most of our lives. My point is that we trust him."

Hannah stopped chewing, a sinking feeling growing in the pit of her stomach. "Where's Ayden?"

"Ayden is gone. Kenny is going to be part of our protection detail."

Hannah composed herself, feeling the scrutiny of both Everly and Kenny. She crunched on bacon and stared at her plate. She was so nailed already. They both had to know…something was going on between her and Ayden.

Something forbidden.

"Will Ayden be back?"

"Kenny, could you give us a moment?" Everly came around to sit on the stool next to Hannah while the man marched across the room and stepped right out the door like a good little soldier.

Hannah bristled at Everly's need to control. Or protect. She would obviously see herself as protecting her brother.

"You and I had this talk yesterday about Ayden. I don't want to see him hurt. Kenny is going to help so that Ayden can get some space and clear his head."

"Was that his idea or yours?" Oh. Had she really just said that? After all, at any moment, they could simply stop protecting Hannah and her mother. She had never asked for their help, but she did appreciate it, given the very real danger.

Everly drew in a breath. "It doesn't matter whose idea it was. It's needed. When I got here last night, I sensed something had changed between you two. I don't know what exactly happened, but I don't like what's going on. I like you, Hannah. I think you're a good person. Whatever happened between you and my brother before… I don't blame you, but I know you still care about Ayden."

She nodded. Everly was right. She hated to admit it but she already knew the truth. "Thank you, for being such a good sister. You're right to bring Kenny here. I wouldn't want to hurt Ayden."

But she might have already, considering the pain radiating through her own heart at what could never be.

* * *

Fisting his hands, Ayden stood in the hallway, listening. He'd come back this morning, his composure in place after the mistake he'd made kissing her, and his day planned out in his mind. He noted both Kenny's vehicle parked in the front and Everly's. Last night, Ayden had taken the rental car back to the office and returned it early this morning with Caine's help. He was in his own vehicle this morning. Bigger. Better. Safer.

Caine took care of the situation with his buddy who had loaned them the van for this safe house transfer. Ayden had considered looking into their own similar vehicle that they could switch out with various company names, if needed. He hadn't imagined his protection services would turn into a similar operation as when he protected high-value assets with the DSS.

But Hannah was high value to someone besides her mother.

Or him.

And he didn't appreciate Everly putting herself between the two of them.

If he hadn't decided to walk around and do a perimeter check, then slip in through the back door as kind of a test to their alertness, he wouldn't have heard the conversation. The alarm was off since they were coming and going.

He moved to the kitchen and stood there until

he caught Everly's attention and then he let the anger spill from his gaze.

She shifted back, her eyes wide. But he wouldn't discuss this with her now in front of Hannah.

"We have work to do," he said.

His sister began cleaning up dishes in the sink. To avoid looking at him?

"I thought you weren't coming back today," she murmured. "Why is Kenny here then, if not to take your place?"

"The investigation is ramping up."

Everly paused and turned to finally look at him, her hands in a sink of soapy dishwater. Hannah set her fork on her empty plate—good, she'd gotten a decent breakfast—and her green eyes hovered on him. She blinked and a blush spread up her neck and cheeks, and he knew exactly what that was about. Memories of their kiss flooded him too and wiped out whatever he would have said next.

And all this right in front of Everly. *Not good.*

"I didn't expect to see you here." His sister cleared her throat. "Has something happened with the investigation?"

"Yes, there have been some new developments." Avoiding her gaze, he moved to the coffeepot, grabbed a mug hanging from a mug tree, and poured a big steeping cup of very black and strong coffee. His sister knew how to make it the way they all needed it, as did Brett. It was a toss-up between the two in terms of their coffee-making skills.

He took a long drink and almost burned his tongue. By the time he was ready to turn around, Hannah had thrust her dish in the sink to wash it, and Kenny had come back in.

He moved to the counter. "I see you're back."

Ayden wanted to bring up the fact that Everly shouldn't have missed that Ayden had come in the back door. Her cell should have at least alerted her of the entry via the motion-detector cameras. They still had much to talk about and ramp up in their protection services. But that was just one reason he would stay here and she would go.

"Yes, I'm here now. Everly is going to head back to the HPS facilities and monitor things from there. She'll be manning the command center."

His sister's eyes widened. "Oh, really. Is that what we're calling it now?"

"I think it works, don't you?" He sipped more coffee, hoping he wouldn't get an argument from her. They had more important things to discuss, but he braced himself for the inevitable.

"I can stay here with Hannah, Ayden," Everly said. "I'm sure she would feel more comfortable with another woman here."

"There's nothing to discuss here. The decision has been made. Caine and Brett have also been informed. As to what's happened with the investigation, Detective Mann has ID'd the man leading the attacks on the hotel and the bank building. Well, let's say they have found a couple of aliases on him, but we'll go with Hamish Grimsson. We'll have to dig deeper to find his true identity. A BOLO alert has been issued on him."

"Can I see the image?" Hannah asked.

"I'll bring it up on my laptop." He set his computer on the counter and opened it. The image popped up to reveal a tall man with dark hair and bushy dark brows, dressed in black. The two men with him wore masks. But he'd lost his or hadn't worn it."

"He's a hit man for hire, then," Everly said.

"And someone hired him to come after you." Kenny looked at Hannah.

"But we still don't know why." Everly's gaze had also fallen on Hannah.

Ayden felt the sudden need to step in front of her. "I don't know if it's as simple as all that."

"What do you mean?" Kenny asked.

Ayden glanced between the retired cop and Everly as he spoke. "Our focus is to protect Hannah and her mother, at all costs, all while we assist the police in finding and apprehending this

Hamish character. Uncovering the reasons behind the incidents can help us with protection. Solving this investigation is part of the protection plan, as long as we stay within the parameters of the law and don't intrude on the investigation."

He was so grateful for the connections he had because of his father, Judge Pierson Honor, and his mother, Special Agent Clair Honor. "So, Everly, go back to the command center and use all our resources to track him, while you're keeping a pulse on protection services."

"Fine," she said. "I'll just go up and grab my small duffel. I guess I'm taking your vehicle back, so you'll need to rely on Kenny."

"Caine is here to pick you up."

"What? Why didn't he come in?"

"He just drove up." Ayden held up his cell with the camera images. "I don't want everyone coming and going because we risk giving away the safe house. Kenny is staying for the long term. I'll go when needed to find answers."

Maybe he could turn this disaster of a job completely around and help bring justice for Stevens's death while protecting Hannah.

And then hopefully he could finally let go of her. They had their one last kiss.

And he had closure. Didn't he?

EIGHTEEN

Kenny had moved outside to check the woods, while Ayden set up a workstation on the table. Hannah wished he hadn't confiscated her laptop. He was worried that someone could trace her through it. Ayden wouldn't even allow her to use a new laptop because looking at emails or opening other accounts could allow someone with the right skill set to find her, and he didn't want to take the risk.

So she was left to find something else to do besides twiddle her thumbs. She perused the bookshelf filled with old paperback novels. Thrillers, spy novels, no romance novels. Too bad.

Still, she had enough trouble with her love life, or her lack of a love life. Make that a *complicated* love life. She tugged a novel out and read the back. If they didn't take out the bad guys quickly, this could be a long, agonizing stay. She wouldn't allow them to keep her separated from her mother more than a week.

Please, God, let it end soon.

Ayden hadn't said much to her at all and seemed completely consumed by whatever he was looking at on his computer. She trusted the screen that had captivated him had everything to do with the investigation. She hadn't wanted to say anything in front of Everly and Kenny, not until she was sure, but that Hamish Grimsson guy looked familiar.

His face could very well feel familiar because she'd seen him that night, escaping up the stairwell, and nothing more.

Hannah tucked the thriller novel back on the shelf. She had enough thrills going on in her life right now, thank you very much. Drawing in a bolstering breath, she made her way to the dining room. Ayden didn't glance up from his laptop.

"I don't mean to distract you, but is there anything I can do to help? Like if you were to get me a new laptop, maybe I could log in to Greenco and search for answers that way."

"I've already explained that someone could trace you that way. There will be no logging in." He finally looked up, his brown eyes darker than usual. They were grim and cold until he exhaled long and slow as though banishing his frustration, then his eyes warmed. She got the sense that he'd come to a decision.

About her, no doubt.

She pulled up a chair. "I get it. Being here with me is hard on you. You'd prefer to be somewhere else. That's why I don't get why you didn't allow Everly to just stay instead of you. You'd be free of me."

Hurt flashed in his gaze. "Is that what *you'd* prefer? Everly instead of me?"

"Wow, you don't pull any punches, do you?"

"I don't see the point in dancing around the issues." He shrugged. "And in my case, it's better if I simply face them head-on."

"I'm the issue you're facing head-on, aren't I?"

His serious expression shifted. His eyes sparkled and his lips quirked, then he chuckled. "I'm sorry. This isn't a laughing matter."

"Then why are you laughing?"

"I heard the teasing in your voice. Make that taunting. You're not *the* issue, Hannah, but protecting you is my task and I'm going to see it through. My sister…she would protect you with her life, too." He dropped his hands in his lap and looked away as if searching for words. Then he found them and looked back at her, this time his eyes holding hers. "You never answered me about your preference."

"And now who's taunting?"

Ayden's cell phone triggered an alert. He glanced at it and palmed his weapon, but then relaxed. Kenny stepped into the dining room. "Did I interrupt something?"

Great. Did everyone already know that she and Ayden once had a thing? Or did the tension hanging in the air give away their secret?

"Nothing at all," Ayden said. "Everything clear?"

"Yes."

"Until this is over, we'll trade out checking the perimeter and the woods—every half an hour. You got that?"

"Yes," the other man replied. "I'm going to get a bottle of water from the fridge. Anyone need something?"

"No," Ayden and Hannah said simultaneously.

Kenny had interrupted them and she was grateful, because she wasn't certain what answer she would give Ayden. Of course she preferred him, and when he wasn't here she worried about him. Longed to see him. Anytime a knock came at the door she was disappointed if it wasn't Ayden. But she knew better than to give in to her feelings for him, so her preference should be Everly over Ayden. *Mind over heart.*

That hardly ever worked.

"Listen, there's something I need to tell you," she said.

With the words, she thought of the secret she kept from him.

Did he deserve to know? Or would it make any difference in his life now, except to hurt him and bring him pain?

Hannah didn't want to bring more anguish to his life than she already had.

"I'm listening." Though he still wanted to know who she would prefer. Then again, maybe not. If she chose him, well, that would trip up his heart. And if she preferred Everly's company, that would also cause him pain for no good reason. They had been over and done for many years, and he'd already made the decision that he could actually move on, though he still didn't know why she'd broken it off with him. But he also realized he didn't need to know that in order to move on.

She hesitated, then, "Can you pull up that picture again?"

He had the distinct impression that she had been about to say something entirely different. "You mean of Hamish?"

"Yes."

Ayden brought the image up as she moved to sit closer to him. He smelled the apple shampoo in her hair, and the scent caused a rush of memories and a surge of emotions from their shared kiss.

He subtly leaned away and hoped she didn't notice.

"Is this the only picture?"

"The only one Detective Mann sent me. I'm logged into to the HPS network and I'm using a prototype facial recognition software to search." He looked at her. She had no makeup on, and he caught the light smattering of freckles across her nose and cheeks, as if the sunlight spilling into the room had brought them to life. "Why did you ask to see this?"

Her eyes narrowed, and lines appeared between her brows. "I'm not sure, but I think I might have seen this man before."

Interesting.

"Are you sure you're not just remembering the night at the office? The same night from which this image is taken?"

She pursed her lips as her frown deepened. "Maybe, but I'm not sure. I'll keep thinking about where I might have seen him."

"It's possible that he had been following you or Stevens, scoping the building out. Maybe he switched to the press release conference to attack there instead."

"Can you pull up security footage at the bank building for the time before the hotel incident?" she asked. "Maybe that'll tell us something."

"I'll talk to Lincoln…although I suspect he's

already looking at it." What seeing the man at the bank building in the days or weeks before would tell them, he wasn't sure. But maybe the guy had a bank account there under another alias for the purpose of having a reason to come and go at the bank as he made his plans. Ayden would communicate his theories to Lincoln.

Other thoughts fought for attention as well. Hamish was an assassin and therefore a marksman. He would assume the same for the two who'd been with him at the Greenco offices. But at the hotel Ayden was sure he'd shot someone. Had there been another assassin at the hotel, who Ayden had shot and injured? Regardless, if the men had wanted Hannah dead, she should already be dead. Possibly Ayden too because he would have protected her, shielded her with his body. So maybe Hamish hadn't wanted to off her quite yet. Or had he missed? Even the most perfect marksmen could miss, especially during the chaos that ensued at the hotel and then at the bank building, where he'd never gotten a real shot at Hannah.

"What are you thinking?" Her soft voice broke through his thoughts.

"Just working it out in my head. It seems that Hamish might need something from you but will take you dead or alive."

"Well, that's comforting?" She shot him a look. A scared look.

He hadn't meant to say the words so bluntly and hated that he'd put that look of fear in her eyes. Ayden wished for her smile again. Her lovely smile. And those lips…

Move on, Ayden. "I have some questions for you."

"I thought I'd already answered them all," she said.

"Not all of them. I never asked these because I thought they might fade away and become irrelevant. But they persist."

"Go ahead and ask then."

An elusive emotion skittered across her face as his eyes locked with hers, but he refused to let it deter him. "Well, first off, thank you for sharing your dream with me about getting your degree," he began. "Sounds like you worked long and hard and finally made it into a high-level position as Stevens's administrative assistant."

She snorted a laugh. "Yeah."

"Why do you keep doing that? You said yourself no one was closer to him—knew his schedule and his appointments. You screened everyone. They came through you first. You knew enough to know his logins, and I assume you sat in on all his meetings, even with engineers and programmers and scientists. You're smart, Hannah. You were the right person for the job. Don't be self-deprecating."

She frowned.

He hadn't meant to upset her but rather to encourage her. He wouldn't ask his question, after all. It had no merit. But she studied him as if reading his mind, and her lips slightly parted.

"Wait. You don't think I was qualified, do you? You think… That's what you want to know. You want to know why *me*? Why I was selected as his assistant. That's it." Hurt rose in her eyes then she blinked it away.

He pursed his lips. Should he deny it? "At first, yes, I wondered. But I'm not questioning your skills. Just…"

"My experience. I was right out of college with an MBA but not actual work experience, though that rarely happens. Then at Greenco, I worked in the reception area for two years, then six months ago I was brought in to train."

"The woman who trained you…"

"Kristen. As I mentioned before, she was pregnant and wanted to train someone else to be there while she was on maternity leave. She planned to come back. Now, of course, we're both out of that particular job. Unless someone steps in to take Mr. Stevens's place, but I can't think of Greenco without thinking of him. He *was* the company, if that makes sense."

But he had a board of directors and investors, Ayden knew, so someone would have to take over. A company didn't have to die because the founder died. That wasn't how businesses worked. Usually.

"Are you sure she would have come back? After she trained you, what was the plan? Where would you be placed in the company next after Kristen returned?"

"To my shame, I hadn't considered that. I was just so thrilled for the opportunity."

"We've gotten a bit off track here. Let's go back to your experience." He rubbed his forehead. "Do you think someone else would have been more qualified?"

"Sure. Lots of people had been there longer than me. I wondered about that at first. Why me? Then I just accepted it. But you know how it is."

"I do. A new person gets the promotion, and someone else with more years and experience is passed over."

She shrugged. "Kristen liked me. She struck up conversations with me at lunch. We hit it off and clicked."

"So she was the one to pick you as her replacement."

"I guess so. What's your angle?" Hannah asked.

He stared at the image on his computer, then closed the file. "To be honest, I'm not sure. Just covering every single base." But if Hamish was after something, maybe he was chasing the wrong assistant. Hannah hadn't been in that position that long.

"I think I'll go grab some water now, and also think about lunch. Need anything?"

"Water would be nice," he said. "I'd say we could call for takeout, but not out here. You don't have to cook for us, Hannah. In fact, I'll take care of lunch. I make a mean turkey sandwich."

She laughed, sending him that smile he loved, then headed for the kitchen for water.

"Remember," he called, "I'm making lunch. Don't you dare touch anything."

"Don't worry. I'm looking forward to seeing if your sandwich lives up to expectations," she called back.

He smiled inside, loving the banter. And yeah, unfortunately, the flirting. He scraped a hand down his face. *What am I going to do, God?*

He wasn't sure what he was going to do about Hannah personally, but he knew what he would do next regarding the case. He sent Everly an email to look into Kristen's background. In the meantime, he would also visit her and ask a few questions.

NINETEEN

Hannah startled awake on the sofa. Ayden stood over her with an unreadable expression.

She shifted to sit. "I can't believe I fell asleep."

"I can. You needed the rest."

After Ayden had made them sandwiches—and he hadn't been kidding, they were fantastic—she'd gotten comfy on the sofa with the thriller novel, after all. It might have been thrilling, but not enough to keep her awake. Considering all she'd been through, it wasn't a fair assessment of the novel.

Where was it anyway?

She spotted it in his hand.

"You must have dropped this." He set it on the coffee table then sat next to her on the sofa.

She fought the need to lean into him. To rest against his shoulder and get comfortable against his chest. Ayden had that effect on her. She wanted to cozy up close to him, soak up the protection and security pouring off him. Never mind about his corded muscles, strong and sinewy, or the angled scruffy jaw. He'd been clean-shaven all the time when she'd dated him before.

She swallowed and refocused her thoughts away from him.

"I'm glad you're here, Ayden. I can't thank you enough for all you've done. Protecting us like this. I would already be dead if it wasn't for you."

She slowly lifted her gaze to find him looking at her. She got caught up in those brown eyes again. They held such depth, intelligence and… uh, oh…longing.

No, no, no. You can't do this. Don't fall again.

Funny. She thought he might be having the exact same thoughts.

"Listen…" he said.

"Oh, no. What's happened?"

After he hesitated, he took her hands in his. "Nothing bad has happened. Your mother is fine. I get frequent updates from Caine. I just wanted to let you know that I'm working with Everly on tracking down a few clues and I need to leave. But Kenny is here, and I'll be back as soon as I can."

"But what is this about? What new information have you learned?" Did this have anything to do with his line of questioning regarding Kristen?

"I'll tell you when I get back." He seemed to

hover there, close to her. His gaze traveled down her face and lingered on her lips, then abruptly his gaze flicked back up to her eyes.

She got the sense that he wanted to kiss her again. Kiss her goodbye before he left. Or at least leave a peck on her forehead as he released her hands and stood from the sofa.

"It'll be over soon," he said. "I have that feeling. Stay inside and away from the windows. Don't stand at the window and look at the mountain just because I'm not here to stop you." He grinned and winked.

Then walked away, leaving her with that image. That memory. The moment she looked outside at how the moonlight silhouetted Mt. Rainier, and then Ayden had come up behind her, and wrapped his arms around her waist and pulled her close. She closed her eyes.

It was the perfect moment.

The calm before the storm of that kiss.

Her heart pounded with those thoughts. She knew she had to think about something else and decided to call her mother. It was strange not seeing Momma every day. Maybe Caine and Brett were keeping her safe, but they didn't know her like Hannah. Her mother wasn't always forthcoming with how she was feeling. Hannah could sense the changes and even know what Momma needed before she did.

She frowned, hating every moment they were apart. She had no idea how much longer her mother would be here, before moving on to her next life in the arms of Jesus. The need to talk to Momma drove her from the sofa. She ran upstairs for the burner phone she'd been given to use to contact her mother.

It wasn't on the side table or in the drawer, on the desk or under the bed. Or in the bathroom. What happened to it? She searched her purse and found only her cell that she kept turned off.

What if Everly had taken the burner and meant to exchange it with a new one? That would seem like something she would do. Hannah's mood quickly sank. She just wanted to hear Momma's voice and make sure she was okay.

Turning on her own cell could potentially allow whoever was after her to locate her. But it wasn't a sure thing. They would have to be constantly monitoring her calls.

It'll be over soon.

Law enforcement had identified the man and were searching for him even now.

Hannah turned on the phone. She'd make it quick—and tell Everly she needed her burner phone back so she could call her mother. Hannah sent a quick text.

She started to turn the cell off when a call came through.

She answered. "Kristen?"

"Oh, Hannah. I'm so relieved! I've been try-ing to reach you. I'm so glad I caught you." She sounded upset.

"What's the matter? What's happened? Is the baby okay?"

"What? Oh, yes, fine. Everything's fine. Lis-ten… I know something. I figured something out. I think I can identify Alfred's killer."

"Actually, we already have the picture of him."

"I have more than a picture. I have motive. I can't… I can't do this on the phone. Meet me somewhere?"

Hannah wasn't about to tell Kristen she was at a safe house and her protector wouldn't agree to a meeting, either. But then again, he was des-perate to know the answers, too—the answers could end all of it.

She would be back with Momma during her last weeks and months. She and Ayden wouldn't have to see each other anymore.

Finding the motive could be a game changer and lead them to the man. "We'll work some-thing out. I'll contact you soon."

"Make it soon. This is urgent. I have to go. Call me."

Kristen ended the call.

Pulse pounding in her head, Hannah turned off her cell, with sweaty, trembling fingers. She'd taken longer than she'd intended, and someone could track her on her phone, according to Ayden. So she wouldn't call him on her cell about the conversation with Kristen. Maybe when Kenny came back in, she could use his cell to contact Ayden to tell him the news.

Her heart pounded with excitement, the hope that this would end soon. Ayden had said he felt like it was going to be over soon. That was all good.

But it would also mean she would have no reason to see him again and her time with him would be over. It would be a painful, bittersweet ending to the biggest trial of her life.

Ayden gripped the wheel, hating to leave Hannah behind. She was a full hour and a half away from him now, but he trusted Kenny to protect her. The man had ample experience. He would be smart and capable if trouble found them at Base Camp. But no one knew Hannah was at the cabin. With the images and at least two aliases found, a BOLO alert given, it sounded like their mystery hit man was on the run and authorities were closing in.

If he was smart, he would be running for his life and hiding away somewhere, not chasing Hannah.

But he would not put all his eggs in the proverbial basket. He would not assume this was over and would continue to pursue answers that could end the danger to Hannah.

Ayden wanted to know more about Stevens and since Kristen had worked for him for years, she could have answers that Hannah didn't have. Ayden hadn't considered talking to her, neither had Lincoln, because she was already home on bed rest and out of the picture when the first incident happened at the conference center, so she hadn't been a priority to question.

He pulled up at the curb to Kristen's luxury home. She was supposedly bedridden the last few weeks of her pregnancy, so he would expect her husband or someone else to be home as well, taking care of her needs. He admired her for sticking with the bed rest to protect her baby and hoped he wouldn't cause her too much stress.

But he needed answers.

He walked up the sidewalk, taking in his surroundings. Nice quiet neighborhood. Flowerpots boasting well-tended flowers, and beautiful landscaping all around. A green yard with a sprinkler system. She obviously paid a landscaper, unless, of course, her significant other enjoyed gardening.

Ayden knocked on the door, mentally preparing his list of questions.

No one answered. He knocked and rang the

doorbell several times, then walked around and peeked into the car garage. Empty.

If Kristen was home, she wasn't coming to the door. He hoped she didn't need help.

At the end of the sidewalk, he frowned and looked up and down the street. He needed to talk to her and didn't imagine that her helper would leave her alone too long, so maybe he should wait here until they returned.

Had any of them considered that Kristen could have been a target, too—because of what she knew? His pulse increased as he drew his cell out and called Lincoln. Someone needed to check on the woman.

He ended up leaving a voice mail. Ayden got back into the SUV and decided to see if he could speak with Lincoln while he was in town. He could learn something that way as well.

A call came through from Everly and he answered.

"I got something, Ayden. You're not going to believe this. Kristen isn't pregnant."

He hadn't heard correctly. *"What?"*

"She's not pregnant."

"What do you mean? Did she lose the baby?" His chest constricted. He pulled the SUV over into a shopping mall parking lot. This conversation would require more focus.

Everly growled. "Kristen claimed to be pregnant, but she was *faking*. Now do you understand?"

The news was a sucker punch to the gut. He let his mind wrap around the information. "I understand. But I'm not sure what it means."

"It means she lied about being pregnant the entire time and therefore her reason for taking maternity leave early is bogus."

Hmm. This news was entirely unexpected. "How do you know this information?"

"You told me to look into her. I sat along the street in front of her house while I used my laptop to look into her life. All I had to do was watch her house for a few hours, and I caught her without a baby bump. None at all."

"And you're sure she didn't already have the baby?"

Everly huffed loud enough for Ayden to hear her frustration. "I'm positive."

"Why would she fake a pregnancy?" His heart pounded. "Hannah."

"That was my thinking, too. This could have everything to do with what's going on. It's too much of a coincidence, and no one feigns a pregnancy without a good reason. Or maybe a sinister reason."

"Right. Kristen picked her. Hired her to be her replacement. Trained her to take her place when she was on maternity leave."

"But we still don't understand why."

"I'll let you do some more digging into her connections, her comings and goings so you can find the reason why. You did a great job, Everly. Thank you. I just left Kristen's house by the way, and she's not there. Her car isn't there if she is."

"Where are you going now?"

"I'm heading back to the safe house. I never should have left Hannah. I have a very bad feeling about this. Please call Kenny for me and tell him to be on alert. Tell Lincoln what's going on, too."

"You got it."

He ended the call and accelerated, determined to get back to Base Camp in record time. He'd had a feeling it was all about to end. A deep gut feeling he should have stayed there with Hannah.

I should have heeded that instinct earlier today. But I was trying to be professional.

Everly had been right—being with her was too much of a distraction, and now he feared his lack of focus may cost Hannah her life.

TWENTY

Hannah crept down the stairs in search of a snack. She would have to give Everly a list of foods. Oreos. Cheetos. Everything she could eat that was wholly bad for her. After all, if she was going to get stuck here with nothing much to do, she would need the comfort food.

Heading to the kitchen, she paused when she noticed Kenny sitting on the sofa. Good, she'd meant to ask him if she could use his cell. He'd been doing a perimeter check, and so Hannah had taken another nap. She felt ridiculous, but she was so tired. But her exhaustion had everything to do with this sudden violence encroaching on her life this week, so she shouldn't feel too guilty.

She started toward Kenny but before she took another step, she realized something wasn't right with him.

He sat deathly still. Unmoving.

Usually he paced, walked around the perimeter, communicated with the HPS team.

A cold chill crawled over her. She continued slowly forward, watching him as she moved. His eyes were closed.

"Kenny? You all right?"

He didn't look up at her. Instead he slumped over on the sofa.

A yelp lodged in her throat but didn't escape. She should run to him. Check on him. Something. But it was as if her feet had melded with the tile floor. She couldn't move. *What is happening?*

"Hannah, Hannah, Hannah…" a mocking voice said.

Surprised to hear the familiar voice, she turned.

Kristen stepped into view from behind the wall separating the kitchen and living room.

None of this was computing. "Kristen? What are you doing here? Are you okay? I told you I would call you and let you know where we could meet."

Hannah relaxed, only a little, and forced a smile, then she took two steps forward. "What is it that you wanted to tell me, now that you're here. You said you had urgent news that would tell us about the motive behind everything. Who is behind it."

Kristen laughed.

Something wasn't right. She wasn't herself.

Hannah glanced down to her midsection. The baby…she'd lost the baby? Oh, no…then that could explain why she was here and acting strange. Still, wariness crept over her. She glanced at Kenny, wanting to check on him, but her neurons were definitely not firing right. Hannah was frozen in place.

"Interesting… I thought you would want to check on your friend."

"Yes, Kenny…" Suddenly her brain unscrambled, and she ran to Kenny. "Kenny! Are you okay?"

But he couldn't hear her because he was dead. She found her voice and pushed beyond the fear and terror keeping her prisoner. The puzzle pieces fell in place.

"What did you do?" She whirled around and glared up at Kristen.

"Oh, come on, he's not dead. He's only sleeping." Kristen brought her arm around from her back and revealed a dart gun.

Hannah found his pulse. Strong. *Thank You, Lord.*

But she didn't understand. She'd known Kristen for over a year. Had grown close to her. They'd been friends. Kristen had taught her everything at Greenco. "What's going on? What happened to...the baby?"

"We don't have much time, but I like you, Hannah. I've always liked you. I didn't mean for things to turn out this way. So I'll tell you what's going on...because we're friends. Though I suppose we won't be after you hear what I have to say."

Hannah considered the layout of the house. The woods.

Kristen was poised on the edge of the sofa with her dart gun. Interesting that she didn't seem to want to kill anyone, though Hannah feared the incidents were all linked. Hamish and Kristen? What was the connection? None of it made sense.

Hannah slowly eased onto the opposite sofa. Kristen hovered over Kenny as if she would dart him again if he moved.

"I'm listening," Hannah said. *Please, come back, Ayden. Please come back to me.*

If he had never left, Kristen wouldn't be here now. She would never have gotten past Ayden. Of that, Hannah was sure.

The woman pressed a hand against her midsection. "I'm sorry about my ruse. I was never pregnant."

"Why would you pretend—"

"Shh." Kristen held a finger to her lips. "Remember. Not much time. You might not know that Alfred and I—I used to call him *Al*—had been working together for years. Al was in the position he was—head of the company about to go public—because I put him there. I was the brains behind Greenco, the ideas, and the proprietary software. I know, you thought I was just his glorified secretary. But *I* should have been the CEO. When I found out that he planned to fire me I pretended to be pregnant and told him it was his."

Hannah gasped. "You were having an affair with him?"

"He was getting out of hand, pulling away. I had to control him somehow."

Hannah closed her eyes and tried to rein in the panic. When she opened her eyes, Kristen was pacing. Restless. Anxious.

"Your plans obviously went wrong."

"I had nine months to put my plan in motion. I found you. Brought you in to train you to take my place. Sort of. Then planned to lie low. You were supposed to be my person on the inside, close to Al. You could do the job, and well, but you still wouldn't catch on because it would literally take years for you to catch up to where I was, to have the knowledge I had. Plus, you're…you're naive. You wouldn't suspect me. You wouldn't see through my scheme."

Hannah tried not to bristle at the insult, because it was insignificant, and what did she care in the grand scheme of things? The fact was, Kristen had let jealousy and greed destroy her reason. If she'd had reason, a sound mind, to begin with, Hannah couldn't know. But she did know that Ayden had suspected something was off with Kristen, and that's why he'd been questioning Hannah. He'd been spot-on.

"Why? You still haven't explained why you would go through all this trouble."

"Because Alfred had hidden the proprietary information that belonged to me. He was planning something. I had to be smart."

Kristen came around the sofa to stand in front of Hannah. She stared down at her.

"He started to suspect something, and I threatened him. I threatened to tell his wife about the baby. He beat me to the punch and told her instead. He took my one bit of leverage away."

"So…what…you hired a hit man?"

Kristen nodded. "They're easy to find online. Mercenaries. Hit men. Assassins. Let them do the dirty work." Kristen held up the dart gun.

"You suspected he was not going to announce the company was going public, didn't you?"

"I knew him too well. He was changing the game on me. Alfred Stevens could never be taken down by a scandal, and having an affair, getting me pregnant was definitely a scandal and too much for him. He withdrew what he needed, the proprietary software…gutting the company, basically. He thought he could start over and launch his own company without me. He would strip me of everything."

"And you didn't expect that curve ball," Hannah said.

"It didn't matter because I had already set things in motion to kill him. Hiring armed gunmen to create chaos and take out a few people during a big environmental convention, and it would be months, maybe years, if *ever*, before they discovered the reason behind the bomb threat and shootings. In the meantime, I could get what he'd hidden from me. I was counting on you to get it for me. When the time was right. When things had settled down, depending on how they settled down…"

"You could come back and be CEO and take his place? But then something else went wrong." Just keep her talking. That's all Hannah had to do. Help would be here soon, wouldn't it? After all, the smart house had cameras everywhere. Kenny might have been caught off guard, but Ayden would know this was happening. He would watch it on his phone. Except he could be driving, and hopefully he was pulling up in the driveway and would burst through that door any minute.

Kristen angled her head and frowned as she lowered herself onto the couch next to Hannah. Would she kill her now? Bring in her assassin to do the job? And if Ayden didn't get here in time, then… *Kenny, please wake up!*

"I didn't know that Alfred had hired that bodyguard. I didn't tell the people I hired there would be trained resistance. How could I know? You'd think that skilled mercenaries would go into the job knowing the risks, plan for them. But one of their men was killed during their operation. Now they're out for blood from *me*, because I didn't inform them of a security specialist guarding their target." Kristen gritted her teeth and fearful tears spilled over. "That's just so…dumb."

Hannah held back her incredulous laugh. Hiring men to kill Mr. Stevens was *dumb*. And apparently, a person could hire the wrong assassin, and in this case, it sounded as if it was backfiring on the woman.

Still, she had more questions. "This is all about you and Mr. Stevens. Between the two of you. So why are they after *me*?"

"You can hire people, bad people. Connect on the dark web. But that doesn't mean you can trust them not to turn on you, which is what is happening. I can't possibly pay them for the loss of their trained soldier and friend. Apparently, that was in the fine print. Who reads that anyway? I mean, I'm supposed to know these unspoken rules?" She released a shuddering breath. "I admit I was out of my league when I went searching on the dark web. Now they want the software. So that means I need the USB from you. I know you went there to get information. I saw you on the camera I planted in Alfred's office. I was watching."

Hannah slowly rose. "Then you also know I don't have it."

"What? I saw you—"

"The phones went down. The cameras. Everything. The men came bursting into the building and into his office. Did you see that part? The bodyguard he hired saved me, but the USB drive was still on the desk. I don't know if I downloaded the software specifically, just files. Lots of files."

"Those files could have some or part of the software, but if they're still after you, that can only mean one thing." Kristen pressed her fingers against her temples. "They didn't get what they wanted and are going to kill me." She slid her gaze to Hannah. "And that means they're going to kill *you*. I came here to save your life.

To prevent them from killing you by giving them the USB with the software."

Hannah shook her head. "You're not making sense."

"They think you're me. I made a mistake and told them I was Alfred's new assistant. That was my first mistake."

No. Not even close.

"I should have told them nothing, not even the reason why I needed him taken out, but it was important for them to understand the scenarios," Kristen explained. "I wanted it to look like someone had targeted the environmental group. Bottom line, they believe you were the one to hire them."

"But they tried to kill me the day they killed Alfred. They shot at me and have been pursuing me ever since."

"Maybe you're mistaken and their pursuit that first day was all part of the chaos, and you had some close calls. I only know that after the bodyguard shot one of their men, everything shifted. They contacted and warned me. If only I could complain about their tactics and warn people on social media." Kristen laughed.

Hannah pressed her hands over her eyes. None of this had a thing to do with her. "How could you do this, Kristen? Getting your hands on the software you supposedly created was not worth everything you've set in motion. Certainly not a man's life." Had Mr. Stevens realized the extent to which she would go? That the woman would go so far as to hire someone to kill him? He must have suspected she would try something because he'd hired Ayden.

A sound jingled. "What's that?" Kristen whirled.

"It's coming from Kenny's cell." Hannah rolled him over enough to tug the cell out. "The cameras are showing someone on the property, hiking in. They're carrying some scary-looking guns."

She showed the image to Kristen whose eyes grew wide. "The hit man. He's found us!"

Ayden pressed the accelerator to the floor, wishing for more speed. But he couldn't take the curves and switchbacks any faster. Not if he wanted to get there in one piece as well as in time to help Hannah.

Kenny hadn't returned his call.

And the app wasn't alerting him. He hadn't been able to pull up the images of the house. Someone could have inadvertently shut down the smart house app. But he didn't think that was it.

And his gut clenched.

God, please help me get there. Keep Hannah safe.

He knew it. He'd known he shouldn't have left her. But he could trust Kenny.

Out of desperation he tried calling one more time, but he wasn't expecting an answer. Something had obviously happened to Kenny. Everly relayed that she'd taken Hannah's burner cell intending to replace it but forgot to give her another. He'd tried Hannah's regular cell.

Again, no answer.

But he'd had the presence of mind to call the sheriff's offices and ask for someone to please send a squad of well-armed deputies out to Base Camp. They could get there faster than he could. Unfortunately, he hadn't received the kind of response he'd wanted. He would expect them to arrive long before he did and for someone to call him back already. The fact that he hadn't received a call concerned him.

He steered down the bumpy road, pushing through the trees. Branches grabbed his vehicle as if to hold him back from seeing what terror lay ahead. He skidded to a stop in front of the cabin and behind Kristen Mayer's vehicle. Everly had sent the images of the not-so-pregnant woman next to her car that was missing from the garage, and here it sat. Grabbing his pistol, Ayden stepped out of his vehicle and used it for cover. Waited and watched.

It was deadly quiet.

The front door suddenly opened. He aimed his gun, hoping, praying that Hannah would step out and think him crazy. Kenny held a hand to his head then stumbled forward onto the porch.

"They're…gone!" He grabbed onto the post.

Ayden rushed forward and grabbed his friend. He ushered him over to the bench to sit. "What's happened? Where have they gone?"

"A woman knocked and said she was a friend of Hannah's. I closed the door and was about to go up to ask Hannah, before letting the woman in." Kenny winced. "She got me with a dart. Knocked me right out. I came to a few minutes ago and found my cell on the table, but I can't… The cameras are off."

"Come on, let's get you into the house."

A deputy sheriff pulled up as Ayden was assisting Kenny back inside. "I'm okay. I'm okay. Got a splitting headache and my vision is blurred, but I'm alive."

You're fortunate to be alive. He held back his anger at the fact that Kristen had gotten the advantage on Kenny. More security measures, more controls to put in place for the future.

Ayden left the door open and waved the deputy in as he clomped up the steps. "You're just now getting here?"

"Dispatch sent me over to check on the cabin. I was on the other side of the county."

"Great. We have a missing woman. Possibly abducted," Ayden spoke quickly. They could already be too late to make a difference.

The officer pulled out a notepad and pen. "Can I get a description?"

"Kenny, would you mind informing the deputy of what happened? Everything. If I can get the cameras back up, I might learn something. Kristen's car is still here." *Where did you go?*

Did she actually think she could take Hannah out into the woods and kill her? That she wasn't going to be discovered? Ayden tugged out his cell again and still couldn't see the cameras. He rushed to the table where he'd left his laptop and booted it up, then logged into the smart house system, and rebooted. The seconds ticked by along with his agitation. He could at least look upstairs.

Finding Hannah upstairs, sitting in her room having a nice chat with Kristen would make his day. But he knew that wasn't going to happen. Kenny had been attacked for a reason. Still, he had to look for her. Her room was empty. Her cell and purse sat on the dresser.

Her cell.

He grabbed it and turned it on as he went downstairs and found his laptop ready. A glance at her cell told him what he feared. She'd turned it on and taken a call from Kristen, who had been waiting for the moment she could snag Hannah's location.

He dropped into the chair and leaned back, the breath whooshing from him with her name… "Hannah…"

Lord, keep her safe!

The smart house system had booted up and he pulled up the camera app on his cell again. Before someone had shut the electronics down somehow, the cameras had caught everything.

His gut sank.

"It's worse than I thought," he told Kenny. "Hamish and his men are in the woods. And now they're after both Hannah and Kristen. The women took the trail out the back."

"Where does that lead?" his friend asked.

"It's several miles' worth of trails, and of course thousands of acres of woods. They could find plenty of places to hide, but these men are trained to find and kill people."

He headed out to his vehicle and grabbed body armor and tactical binoculars. Stashed extra ammo.

The deputy was back at his automobile too, using his radio to call in backup. He paused and stared at Ayden. "What are you doing? You can't go after them. We need to wait for backup. They're…"

"These men are assassins, and they are not going to wait. *Hannah* can't wait." He slammed the car door. Kenny stood there, waiting for instructions. His eyes still wonky.

"I'm sorry I let you down. I'll come with you. I'll be your backup."

He patted the man on the back as he took off. "You wait here and watch the house for intruders. It's not your fault, Kenny."

Ayden took off into the woods, wary and guarded, but they had half an hour on him, according to the cameras. Body armor wasn't designed for jogging, at least in his opinion, and he struggled to breathe. Sweat poured from him. But he pushed on and up the trail, slowing to a hike. A noise to his left sent him crouching behind a rock.

A deer.

Think, Ayden, think.

Where would they go, even if they *could* escape these men? He hoped and prayed he didn't find bodies along the way, but he searched the woods as he ran, too. At the top of an incline, he climbed onto a rocky outcropping, and pulled out the binoculars. Mt. Rainier was large and intimidating in his view.

He searched…spotted the gondola.

Ayden hopped down and started up the trail

again. They had to be somewhere between here and the gondola, or already on it and riding it up. And Hamish wouldn't be far behind.

TWENTY-ONE

Terror raced through Hannah's veins. She was breathless by the time they had made it to the gondola that would take them to near seven thousand feet on Mt. Rainier, stopping at the highest altitude restaurant in the state. She could think of no other escape at the moment.

"Let's ride this." Kristen apparently had the same idea. "Looks like it's going to leave soon. Let's go."

They purchased tickets to ride the gondola and then waited in a short line. It seemed nonsensical. On the other hand, Hannah wanted to get far away from the men after them. Would the line take too long, though? She glanced over her shoulder. They couldn't have lost those guys. They must be hiding, waiting in the shadows. Would they take both her and Kristen out in front of all these people? Images of the hotel chaos accosted her. Yes. Yes, they would.

Hannah wanted to escape, but Kristen still had

Kenny's gun, which she kept tucked away. She'd tossed the dart gun at some point.

Hannah had been surprised the mercenaries hadn't shot at them in the woods, but maybe they were confident they would catch up to her and Kristen. The men must have plans for them before they killed them, or maybe the plan wasn't to kill them but to sell them to some human trafficking ring. The horrors pounded through her head to go along with the rapid beat of her heart as the gondola line inched forward.

She kept glancing over her shoulder but couldn't see the men. They couldn't be that far behind, could they? Never mind that Kristen had cut the rope bridge after they'd crossed. That had to have slowed them down.

When she stepped onto the gondola and the doors closed, she dropped into the seat. She and Kristen were both breathless. Sweaty and gasping, still, though it had been a few minutes since their long strenuous run for their lives. Unfortunately, they drew a lot of stares and scrutiny. She thought back to the convention center.

The mayhem.

Being here with people on this gondola… "We shouldn't have done this."

Kristen eased into the seat next to her. "What are you talking about?" she mumbled quietly.

"We shouldn't have gotten on the gondola."

Hannah leaned closer. "People could die because of us. Because of me. Because of *you*."

Kristen rubbed her temples. "Look, let's just get to the top—"

"And then what?" Hannah had spoken too loudly and drew another look from an older woman, who pulled her grandson closer.

Hannah waited until conversation started up among the others on the gondola then leaned closer. "I don't have the USB drive. I don't have anything you want or need. So we go our separate ways when we get to the top."

She should have made that call before taking the gondola, but getting away had been her priority. The men could easily have gotten on another one of the cars, but dressed in tactical gear and holding automatic weapons, they might have had to ditch their terrifying appearance first. If they even cared.

"Whether you like it or not, we're in this together," Kristen said. "They will never stop hunting you because they think you're me."

Hannah pursed her lips. Could she even believe this woman? Kristen had gone through with an elaborate plan filled with lies and betrayal—a woman scorned.

"If that's true, then why are you with me? Why not escape the danger?"

Kristen's eyes narrowed. "Quiet. People are staring."

Hannah stood and held on to one of the steel supports, looking at the expansive views of Mt. Rainier and the Cascade Range. She needed a plan.

Realization dawned. Kristen wanted to keep close to Hannah because she knew too much. She'd just confessed everything back at the house—did she realize she was on camera? Maybe not. But now Hannah knew her secrets. Kristen would keep them together, pretend they were escaping the bad guys together, and then she would kill Hannah.

She slid her gaze to the beautiful blonde whom she'd considered a friend. Hannah had been so grateful when Kristen had selected her to take her place. The woman was obviously smart, but somewhere along the way she'd crossed the line. Desperation had pushed her to do despicable things, and now it was all blowing up in her face.

And unfortunately, Hannah's face, too.

She wouldn't doubt that Kristen's elaborate scheme had included framing Hannah for everything.

Could she outsmart this woman?

The gondola doors opened, and she rushed through the crowd, running to the area beyond the lodge—frantic to get away from Kristen and the gunmen she'd hired, if that story could be believed. She had to get a phone. Call for help. All this while not endangering others.

Confusion rocked through her, but only one thing mattered.

Stay alive until Kristen was caught. Until the bad guys were captured. She rushed around behind the café and the lodge. Then looked out at the woods and yet more trails. The wind whipped around her. Though it was summer, it was much colder at this elevation on Mt. Rainier, and she was definitely underdressed. Everly hadn't imagined Hannah would be running for her life on Mt. Rainier.

Neither had Hannah.

Could she survive without getting hypothermia if she had to remain hidden until it was safe? She moved away from the lodge and started down the trail then leaned against a tree near a ledge—an overlook with a panoramic view of the Cascades.

God, I'm too exhausted. I can't run anymore. Help me. You're my strong tower. Please keep me safe.

The barrel of a gun pressed against the back of her head. She moved to twist around and disarm the gun wielder, but Kristen stepped back, putting distance between them. She had the advantage. "I don't want to shoot you. I didn't want it to come to this."

"Please, please. I didn't ask for you to hire me. Let me go. I promise I won't—"

"Shh." The familiar smirk crept into Kristen's lips as she aimed the gun, slowly walking toward Hannah, who backed up. "Now, we both know that's not true. As soon as you had the chance, you would tell the police everything I said. And honestly, I have a failsafe. You look guilty, Hannah. I expect the police are planning to arrest you."

"Then let them. Let them arrest me." With the cameras at the judge's cabin, the truth would come out. An incredulous laugh escaped, and certainly not her first during this whole ordeal.

She was relying on the judge—though deceased—for help? Well, the only person getting her out of this would be herself.

And God, if it was His will. Tears surged as she thought of her mother.

Lord, please don't let my mother go through this. To learn I was murdered and then to die alone.

"Unfortunately, you know too much, even for the failsafe," Kristen said. "I had a soft spot for you and so I told you everything. *Oops.* Now you need to die and I need to escape and disappear. Now…just keep backing up."

Hannah risked a glance over her shoulder.

The sheer drop would kill her. *Is this it, then, Lord?*

Hannah squared her shoulders. Lifted her chin. "You thought I was inexperienced and naive. A pushover you could use. Well, I'm not the weakling you mistook me for. I'm not going to make it easy for you, Kristen. I'm not going to jump. So you're just going to have to shoot me."

The woman growled as she rushed toward Hannah to push her over.

She stepped out of the way at the last moment, and Kristen screamed as she fell from the ledge, but she caught it.

Barely hanging on for her life, her eyes were wide as she begged. "Help me, help me, Hannah, please!"

Heart pounding, she grappled with the unexpected twist of events and dropped to her knees to grab Kristen's hands and pull her back up. Kristen had dropped the gun so that she could hang on with both hands, and now she had no weapon. She was no deadly threat to Hannah. She wouldn't let Kristen die when she could help her, but then she would need to subdue her until the police arrived.

Kristen crawled up onto the ledge gasping in tears. "You saved me, Hannah. Why…why would you do that?"

"I'm not a murderer."

"I wasn't, either. That's why I hired someone else. But I don't want to die, and I don't want to go to prison. I don't deserve this."

"I didn't deserve how you treated me either," Hannah said. A chill crawled over her, and she started to move away from Kristen.

She suddenly shoved Hannah and straddled her with more strength than Hannah could fathom, wrapping her hands around Hannah's throat. "You made the mistake of trusting me again. I'm sorry, Hannah, but you really do need to die."

Kristen squeezed her throat.

Hannah couldn't breathe. She kicked and squirmed, and focused on getting Kristen's hands off her throat.

Darkness edged her vision. She tried to reach for Kristen's eyes to gouge them, but the woman was taller and had longer arms, and Hannah couldn't reach her. She searched for a rock. Something to hit her in the head with. To gain her freedom.

God, help me!

A figure rushed from out of nowhere. Kristen gasped, loosened her grip then fell to the side.

She recognized the figure now. Ayden. He was here.

Ayden lifted her in his arms. "Hannah, my Hannah, are you okay?"

My Hannah...

Heart in his throat, Ayden looked down at her beautiful face, into her beautiful emerald eyes, her auburn hair spilling and curling over her shoulders and his arms. She gasped for breath, her hands moving to her throat as she sucked in air. He wanted to wipe the tears and the fear from her eyes.

"Ayden..." She whispered his name. "I hoped you would come."

He lifted her closer and pulled her to him.

He never should have left her alone, even with Kenny, someone he trusted.

Lord, I could have lost her!

He held her close and tight and rocked back and forth as she sobbed against his shoulder. The county SWAT team rushed forward and surrounded them and took Kristen Mayer into custody. He'd hit her in the head with his gun to knock her unconscious and free Hannah from having the life choked out of her.

Evening was setting in, bringing a rush of serious cold. Neither of them had worn jackets or warm clothing. They would need to get out of here soon. He released her enough to look at her face and lifted her chin.

"It's over, Hannah. Everly called in SWAT, and they captured the mercenaries before they could board the gondola, and now Kristen is in custody."

"They arrested her?" Hannah sucked in a slow breath and released it equally as slowly. She was calming down, composing herself.

She'd been through so much, and he didn't understand why bad things happened, even to good people. At first, he had been furious that he somehow had been caught up in her life again. That first moment in Stevens's office when he'd seen her—he'd been too stunned for words.

Anger and resentment had built up in his chest, but he'd hidden those feelings away. Still, God had seen...

And He'd been the one to bring them together. He always worked things out for good.

The wind picked up and blasted cold over them, dragging hair into her eyes. She shoved it out of her face. "She made it sound like she framed me. That everything was *my* doing. Even hiring those assassins. She claimed she made sure all the evidence would point to me."

The fear in her eyes cut him to the quick. He slipped his hand around her jaw, then slid it up behind her head, weaving his fingers through her hair.

"Don't worry, Hannah. You're not in any trouble. I got her confession on the camera at the house. No one is going to arrest you." A few drops of cold rain reminded him of their predicament. "Let me get you somewhere safe and warm. I think a storm is moving in."

He lifted her in his arms.

"I can walk. You don't have to—"

But he didn't listen to her words, and they faded with the wind anyway. She was trembling. He climbed into the waiting helicopter with her. A crowd had gathered to watch but were now dispersing as the weather moved in.

After instructing the county helicopter pilot where he wanted to land, he buckled Hannah in and secured himself for the short trip to the family cabin.

As the bird lifted off the ground and he peered at Mt. Rainier, which loomed so large in the entire Puget Sound region—it was like a beacon to them all declaring God's majesty. His glory.

How surreal it felt to be flying away, having rescued Hannah from certain death. It didn't take long for the helicopter to land in the clearing at Base Camp. Dad had made sure there was enough space for a helicopter landing. Ayden was surprised his father hadn't also added a helicopter pad, but then again that would completely disrupt the natural setting and serve as a reminder of the very things one wanted to escape when coming to the cabin.

When they landed, he assisted Hannah out and onto the ground, and ushered her inside. Caine and Everly were waiting inside with encouragement, support and a million questions.

Everly hugged Hannah.

Wow. The truth was they'd all grown to love Hannah.

Love… Hannah.

He had to admit that he still loved her. But he would have that one last secret she'd kept from him before he moved in that direction in a serious way. If she even wanted to.

"You can gather your things, Hannah, and I'll take you back to your mother's house. Brett has already taken her home, and she's waiting for you."

"Are we sure it's safe?"

"The men that Kristen hired are in custody. Hamish is already wanted on many other charges, murder of course, but also espionage and selling stolen tech on the dark web."

"And what about Kristen? It's hard to believe she could commit any of these crimes."

Everly stepped closer. "Kristen's father is serving time for embezzlement and kidnapping. Sometimes, the apple doesn't fall far from the tree. I'm just saying…she must have had criminal tendencies, so maybe it's not so surprising she would commit these crimes."

As if that was an excuse for Kristen's actions.

Ayden wished Every hadn't said anything, and he didn't like the look in Hannah's eyes. Was she thinking of her own father? "But obviously not every time."

She gave him a funny look then shuddered and rubbed her arms. "I'll just get my things—what you brought me." She shrugged, looking tenuous, but then a beautiful smile emerged on her face. "I can't thank you enough. All of you."

She climbed up the steps.

Everly turned her attention to Ayden. "I'll take her, Ayden."

"No. I'll be the one."

"Now, wait a—"

"No, *you* wait minute." He stepped closer so he could speak in low tones. "Hannah is my responsibility. All I could think about when she was almost killed was…that I still love her—"

"Which is exactly why you need space. I don't want to see you get hurt again, Ayden."

Arms crossed, Caine stepped forward. "You need to stand down, Everly. Love is always a risk, and I think Ayden might be willing to take that risk."

A few minutes later, Hannah came back downstairs, her beautiful eyes huge and luminous as she looked at his siblings. "I… I probably won't see you again. I don't know how to thank you enough. You all kept me and my mother alive."

She exited the cabin and Ayden followed, turning to glance over his shoulder.

Maybe he should have listened to Everly's warning. Would he also hear her last words to his siblings, spoken to him, personally?

I probably won't see you again.

TWENTY-TWO

After Hannah settled Momma on the sofa with a snack and her favorite television show—like she was a small child—she had to address the big purple beast in the room.

Ayden.

He hadn't left but waited, and the tension in her chest just kept building. She sensed he wanted to talk about more personal issues. On the drive from the cabin back to the house, they had rehashed much of what had happened from the moment Mr. Stevens had hired Ayden, the hotel shooting and bomb threat and everything up to that moment where she'd saved Kristen only to have her turn around and try to kill Hannah again.

She felt betrayed and hurt and just…stunned, frankly. And happy, too, seeing her mother settled into her favorite chair. Friends from church had straightened up the house after the police released the crime scene.

Momma glanced up at her. "Go on now. You and Ayden have a lot to talk about. Don't worry. God took care of us, and He is always there for you. Even in what's between you and Ayden." She winked.

Hannah was surprised her mother seemed to know that there was something between them, or *had* been, and at the moment, wasn't expressing hurt that Hannah hadn't shared with her that she'd been in love.

She was ashamed now at the way she'd handled everything before.

Ayden stood out on the porch staring out over the backyard as if he was standing at a pier, looking out over the water. She sighed and headed that way. Better to get this over with, whatever happened.

She opened the door and slipped out to stand next to him. The moment she was near him, a headiness wrapped around her, and she was once again drawn to him. His protectiveness, his... goodness. Everything about Ayden was good. He'd gone out of his way to safeguard her and Momma, and she knew that he would do it for anyone in need, not just Hannah.

But fear crawled through her. Fear and shame.

He turned to look at her, his intense eyes piercing into her soul, it seemed, and took her breath away. Ayden said nothing at all, just leaned in for a kiss.

And though she shouldn't—she knew what stood between them—she let him kiss her. It would be the very last one—because once she told him what stood between them, he wouldn't want any part of her. His lips explored hers, and it felt as if his heart touched hers, caressing and…loving.

Through his kiss, emotion and longing poured through him, and she sensed he wanted the promise of more.

A deep cry erupted in her throat, and she stepped back.

"Oh, Hannah. Did I hurt you? I'm so sorry, I didn't—"

She pressed the back of her hand to her mouth as the tears surged. "No, it's not that. You didn't hurt me. I did. I hurt us both."

A deep frown shadowed his eyes as he peered at her. And yes, she saw the hurt there. She was hurting him even now. She'd lost him before but now she would lose him forever.

"Why?" The simple word came out, gentle but gruff.

She should tell him the whole of it. If it was only about her, she would have no problem doing so, but it involved his father.

"I need an answer, Hannah. I want us to try

again. To be together again, but if you can't, if you won't, please just give me a reason."

"You won't want me after... I tell you."

"I can't imagine anything changing how I feel about you."

Hannah couldn't tear her gaze from his and knew that he wasn't going to let it rest. Even if the truth crushed him and his family, he had a right to know. Who was she to keep this from him?

She took a step off the porch and found chairs in the yard. The stars were coming out. This should be a romantic reunion, but instead... Hannah told Ayden everything, including the news of his father taking a bribe.

Her heart pounded, palms sweated—would he even believe her about his father, Judge Honor?

He stared up at the stars as if deep in thought, and his features had grown grim. Deep lines around his eyes and mouth made him look so much older. Then he blew out a slow breath and looked at her.

Pain poured from his eyes.

She held her breath. *Oh, Lord, I should have told him long ago.*

"I believe you, Hannah."

She couldn't trust her ears and sat up. "Wait. You believe me?" She hadn't expected it. Hoped, yes. Expected, no.

"I do. There have been questions about Dad's death. His murder. Rumors that he'd taken bribes while on the bench, but no proof. And I believe you might have solved the mystery behind the rumors— No, not rumors. It was the truth."

Her heart leaped for joy, except there was something in his eyes. Regret? Anger? Something held him back. He stood, keeping his distance from her.

"As for you taking the money…" He held her gaze for a few breaths, a few pounding heartbeats, then looked away.

"I tried to do the right thing and return the money but then I overheard your father taking a bribe. And we were about to lose everything. Even so, I knew it was a mistake… I still love you, Ayden. Please, can you forgive me?"

"I'm going to need some time." Then he walked away from her, around the side of the house and disappeared.

Six months later Hannah huddled with Momma as they looked out over the Salish Sea on their dream cruise to Juneau, Alaska. She had landed a new job with a tech company, while a new CEO was put in place at Greenco. Hannah had been offered a well-paying job at Greenco because she'd known so much, but she had decided against sticking with the company where she would be reminded daily of so much bad that had happened. She'd spent a month bringing the new people up to speed on what she knew and had learned from both Kristen and Mr. Stevens. Both had suffered tragic endings, though Kristen still had her life.

Now Hannah worked for an online travel company, and she couldn't be happier.

Momma squeezed her hand. "God is so good, Hannah. Don't you ever forget it."

"I won't, I promise."

Her mother was in remission, even though they'd originally thought she only had a few months to live. She would appreciate every moment with her mother, and this was one big memory they were creating together. A whale breached and the sight left Hannah in awe. More of the passengers gathered along the rail to watch the whales.

Someone moved next to her on the rail. A familiar sensation crawled over her, and the scent… Her skin tingled. She held her breath and didn't overreact in case her imagination was running wild—and the deep hope she'd buried was scrambling to get out when she longed to forget.

"Fancy meeting you here." The deep familiar voice sent warm tendrils curling around her heart.

Ayden.

Too surprised for words, she turned to look

at him, then finally found her voice. "Ayden…
what in the world. What are you doing here?"

"Your mother invited me."

Hannah stepped back from the rail and glanced
between the two, the conspiratorial grins telling
her everything. Her mother was playing match-
maker.

Ayden's cute grin—oh wow, she'd missed
his grin. His face. His dark brown eyes. His
broad shoulders. Everything about him. But he
hadn't been able to live with her betrayal. Had
her mother just ruined their cruise by inviting
Ayden?

His grin shifted, his lips turning downward.
He stepped forward. "Hannah…" He looked to
her mother for, what, a rescue? "I thought…we
thought to surprise you. But if you don't want
me here, I'll disappear. You won't see me again."

Tears rushed to her eyes. "I haven't seen you
in six months. Ever since you walked out and
said you would need time."

He took yet another step forward. "I know.
I'm sorry. I did need time. I took the time…and
I worked through the grief and anger, and now
I'm the one who needs to ask for forgiveness."

Then another step. Now he was close enough
to reach out and take her hand, which he did.

"I can't keep doing this with you. I can't keep
going through the hurt."

He pursed his lips, resolve in his eyes. "And neither can I. Please forgive me for letting what happened before even for one second come between what is happening between us now. The second chance that God gave us. I never forgot about you. I never stopped loving you, and that's why I carried so much hurt for so long. Please, let's not let the bad that other people have done keep us apart."

She glanced at her mother, who remained at the rail as she said, "You've always been braver than you believe, stronger than you seem and smarter than you think, Hannah."

She didn't miss Momma's subtle nod of encouragement. Her mother had known that Hannah wasn't truly happy, even in the midst of all the good that had happened. That her happiness wasn't complete—she pined away for Ayden on the inside.

Regretted her mistake that almost cost her everything.

But here he was, standing in front of her, forgiving her and making amends of his own. "I love you, too, and I won't let anything come between us ever again," she whispered.

Then she took the next step forward and into his arms.

He held her, then released her enough to kiss her again, thoroughly, and full of all the love she wanted and needed. Then he whispered in her ear, "You're the strongest, most beautiful woman I've ever known. Hannah, will you please marry me?"

He stepped back and struggled with something in his pocket, then pulled out a gorgeous emerald cut topaz ring. "This… I was going to give this to you before."

"You kept it all these years?"

He nodded.

"Yes, Ayden, I'll marry you." She sniffled and let him slide the ring onto her finger.

Oooohs and aaahhhhs resounded, only the crowd was captivated by a whale that breached near the cruise ship.

"If this is how our engagement is starting out…" she said.

"You have an amazing future together," her mother finished for her, tears of joy flooding down her cheeks.

And in Ayden's warm brown eyes, Hannah saw the truth of those words.

* * * * *

Dear Reader,

Thank you for reading *High-Risk Rescue*! I hope you enjoyed reading this story as much as I enjoyed writing it. I especially enjoyed the continual reminders from Hannah's faith-filled mother. Her faith was stalwart and I long to be like her. My hope and prayer is that you too are able to remain unwavering in your Christian faith, but for many of us there are times when we struggle to believe. Regardless of those struggles, God never leaves us. He is faithful to us even when we are not faithful to Him. I don't know about you, but that knowledge brings me great joy and leaves me with ample peace.

I love to connect with my readers. Please find out more about me and my books over at my website, ElizabethGoddard.com. There you'll also find ways to connect with me on Facebook, Twitter and Instagram. Sign up for my newsletter to receive monthly updates! I hope you'll join me.

Many blessings!
Elizabeth Goddard

Get 4 FREE REWARDS!

We'll send you 2 FREE Books plus 2 FREE Mystery Gifts.

FREE
Value Over
$20

Both the **Love Inspired®** and **Love Inspired® Suspense** series feature compelling novels filled with inspirational romance, faith, forgiveness, and hope.

YES! Please send me 2 FREE novels from the Love Inspired or Love Inspired Suspense series and my 2 FREE gifts (gifts are worth about $10 retail). After receiving them, if I don't wish to receive any more books, I can return the shipping statement marked "cancel." If I don't cancel, I will receive 6 brand-new Love Inspired Larger-Print books or Love Inspired Suspense Larger-Print books every month and be billed just $5.99 each in the U.S. or $6.24 each in Canada. That is a savings of at least 17% off the cover price. It's quite a bargain! Shipping and handling is just 50¢ per book in the U.S. and $1.25 per book in Canada.* I understand that accepting the 2 free books and gifts places me under no obligation to buy anything. I can always return a shipment and cancel at any time. The free books and gifts are mine to keep no matter what I decide.

Choose one: ☐ **Love Inspired**   ☐ **Love Inspired Suspense**
                  Larger-Print   **Larger-Print**
                  (122/322 IDN GNWC)   (107/307 IDN GNWN)

Name (please print)

Address   Apt. #

City   State/Province   Zip/Postal Code

Email: Please check this box ☐ if you would like to receive newsletters and promotional emails from Harlequin Enterprises ULC and its affiliates. You can unsubscribe anytime.

Mail to the Harlequin Reader Service:
IN U.S.A.: P.O. Box 1341, Buffalo, NY 14240-8531
IN CANADA: P.O. Box 603, Fort Erie, Ontario L2A 5X3

Want to try 2 free books from another series? Call 1-800-873-8635 or visit www.ReaderService.com.

*Terms and prices subject to change without notice. Prices do not include sales taxes, which will be charged (if applicable) based on your state or country of residence. Canadian residents will be charged applicable taxes. Offer not valid in Quebec. This offer is limited to one order per household. Books received may not be as shown. Not valid for current subscribers to the Love Inspired or Love Inspired Suspense series. All orders subject to approval. Credit or debit balances in a customer's account(s) may be offset by any other outstanding balance owed by or to the customer. Please allow 4 to 6 weeks for delivery. Offer available while quantities last.

Your Privacy—Your information is being collected by Harlequin Enterprises ULC, operating as Harlequin Reader Service. For a complete summary of the information we collect, how we use this information and to whom it is disclosed, please visit our privacy notice located at corporate.harlequin.com/privacy-notice. From time to time we may also exchange your personal information with reputable third parties. If you wish to opt out of this sharing of your personal information, please visit readerservice.com/consumerschoice or call 1-800-873-8635. **Notice to California Residents**—Under California law, you have specific rights to control and access your data. For more information on these rights and how to exercise them, visit corporate.harlequin.com/california-privacy.

LIRLIS22

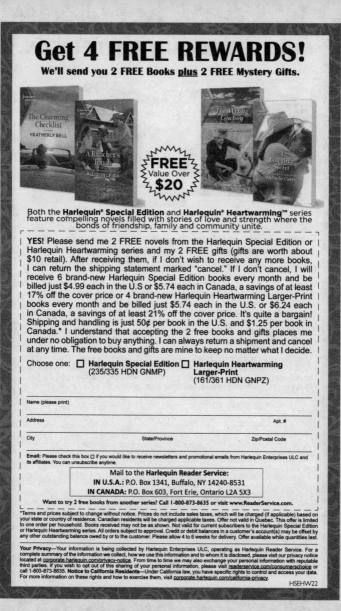